EASY GAME

DR. ESI ELLIOT

Library of Congress Control Number:	2020906627
Paperback:	978-1-952309-65-6
Hardcover:	978-1-952309-66-3
eBook:	978-1-952309-67-0

30 Wall Street, 8th Floor

New York City, NY 10005
www.bookartpress.us
+1-866-257-9368

CONTENTS

CHAPTER 1

Adendo Bilay, General Manager of the Ghanaian Trade Centre, drove with much trepidation up to the gate of his boss, Tenkora Babanda's house to deliver the letter, which Tenkora had sent through the Expedited Mail bag to the office. It was a letter to Mrs. Serena Babanda. The letter had given him an opportunity to see Serena again. He hadn't heard from her for a long time. They hardly spent time talking like they used to now that she was married to Tenkora.

He drove his car through the driveway as the watchman opened the gate for him. It was a huge luxurious house with handsomely carved double doors, vaulted ceilings, marble floors, lofty rooms and luxurious spaciousness. The lamps were turned on in the porch, which was fringed with potted plants everywhere. The beauty of the mansion was lost on him as the voice of the poor farmers resounded in his ears:

"We have not been paid our monthly wages. Thank you does not go to the market!"

"Uncle Dendo, Uncle Dendo!"

"Not so loud, Ayisi." Serena said, walking towards Adendo with the rhythmical movements he found so irresistible. Age had improved, not detracted from her looks. Her beauty seemed more mature, more striking.

He was enthralled as she smiled sweetly at him. He gazed at the light that shone in her eyes, depicting a certain kind of inner beauty - kindness and loyalty. Her arms were wrapped tightly round the chubby little body of Ayisi, her five-year old boy. Ayisi rubbed his face against her arm.

He walked up to her and hugged her. Serena studied Adendo carefully, not able to withhold the inner joy she felt at seeing him. He was taller and thinner and there were lines around his eyes. But he was still Adendo - the determined jaw, and the gentle expression on his face. He was still the same man she had loved several years back.

"You wouldn't believe this." She said as she hugged him back. "I dreamt about you yesterday."

"Did you dream about Agripower as well? Adendo asked "The farmlands are doing well after we are trying that indigenous methods of irrigation."

"Indigenous methods of irrigation?" Serena enquired impressed "That would save the Trade Centre a lot of money."

"We are also saving money with negotiations for the farming machinery"

"Nothing is free. What are you paying back?" Serena studied Adendo with her sharp eyes.

"Transformative Collaboration" Adendo stated emphatically. "When Africa develops, the whole world benefits."

"I wish him well" Serena stated flatly "Fat slave. I would rather starve free."

Adendo suddenly felt uncomfortable "Serena, I have a letter for you from Tenkora."

"A letter?" She asked, surprised, propelling Adendo into the sitting room. "Can I get you something to drink?"

"Nothing. I'm fine. Thank you." He smiled warmly, relaxing further into the comfortable sofa.

"So what's really going on with you?" Serena asked after a while. "Have you heard from Adelina?"

Adendo stiffened at the mention of his ex- wife.

"Oh, she's fine." He quickly changed the topic. "Here is your letter."

Serena slowly and reluctantly opened and read it. Her facial expression changed as she digested the contents. It was a short but brutally honest letter. Tenkora was referring to her 'barrenness' and suggesting that she try certain herbal cures, such as he had heard of in Nigeria. She had no choice, he was saying."

Frozen inside with a mixture of grief, anger and confusion, Serena folded the letter, placing it carefully on the side table and burst into tears.

"Serena." Adendo said alarmed. "What is wrong? What has upset you?"

Serena had to control her sobs at the sound of Adendo's soothing voice.

"Tenkora, he...he wants children" She burst out as if telling a secret she could no longer hide. "We've tried so hard but nothing has happened and he....he blames me." She gasped, her eyes filled with fresh tears. " I have tried all sorts of medical treatment including artificial insemination and now he talks of me visiting Nigeria for herbal treatment."

"We grow herbs on Agripower farms" Adendo Interjected after while. "Maybe we can grow the ones he is talking about" He said jokingly to lighten the tension he was feeling.

Serena laughed "Fertiity herbs? This is possible with the great job you are doing on the farms"

Adendo made a serious face. "But seriously, we are struggling and that is why Adendo has gone to the Global Technology Conference to negotiate for the farming machinery."

"Do not forget that the Western technology should be complemented by indigenous techniques. What if you do not obtain the machinery?" Serena sked as she walked with Adendo inside the house.

Adendo sensed Serena was hurting and put his arms around Serena comfortingly. "I thought you were happy Serena. Don't worry, I will talk to Tenkora when he comes back."

There was an uneasy silence. Serena's hands begun to shake uncontrollably and Adendo grabbed her gently by the wrist.

"Tenkora's family wants him to divorce me." She looked very vulnerable and helpless.

"My goodness!" Adendo exclaimed.

"I know he won't do it. Not because he loves me but because of Dad's property." Serena said sadly.

Adendo was amazed. One who did not adore her was a brute. Her beauty and charm were all there, vibrant and apparent. She had grace in her every step, pose and gesture.

"I feel so confused. When I first married Tenkora, he was so warm......" tears filled Serena's eyes. "Now there is a great deal of friction with very little to show for it, not even a child."

He watched her intently now. For a moment, they stared at each other.

"Why did you stop working Serena? You are so intelligent." Adendo asked, breaking the silence.

"Tenkora wanted me to be a housewife." She stated lamely.

"You must find something to occupy yourself, Serena. Never stop dreaming. One day they may come true."

The words rang chords that struck deep into Serena's heart. It was so easy to be around Adendo. He had warmth that invited easy confidence.

"I've always been able to tell you my problems."

"I remember well." Adendo replied quietly, his mind went back to the closeness they had shared and his heart grew heavy.

"I have to go now." He got up, the rush of emotion too much to bear.

"So soon?" Serena asked. Somehow, she didn't want him to leave.

"Yes'" he said in a whisper. He cleared his throat. "Yes." he said more loudly. He got up and she walked him to his car. He waved as he disappeared out of the gate and then after some hesitation turned back to her. "I will call you tomorrow."

She nodded and waved back.

As Adendo drove off, Serena thought of Tenkora and recalled his cold eyes and composed demeanor, comparing this to the openness and sincerity of Adendo. She wondered what his ex-wife Adelina had been thinking of to walk out on such a fine man.

"Perhaps....perhaps, I should have married Adendo." She whispered to herself suddenly, shocked at the revelations of her own heart.

....

Adendo switched on the radio in his car to calm down but the song that played made him even more confused: She's a black magic woman........

He realised that although he had tried very hard to hide his feelings for Serena, seeing her made him only confirm what he had suspected. He was still drawn to her. He remembered the first time he had met her. It had been under unfavourable circumstances in a luxurious hotel room at the Hotel Charmant in Bendon where he had to work as a manservant to pay his way till his scholarship begun.

He remembered his feelings of degradation as he cleaned out the filth of sloppy occupants and the shouts and jeers of the Housekeepers for petty oversights. It had been the depth of his humiliation when he had been accused of stealing money belonging to an American traveller. Serena who was then a Housekeeper at the Hotel had come to his rescue.

"Mr. Bilay is a very honest member of staff. He is not capable of stealing your money."

"This man looks like he is capable of anything!." The American traveller had sneered.

"Here you are, take your fifty dollars and leave our staff alone. Mr. Bilay, could you please come with me to my office."

They had hit it off immediately. They had chattered away as if they were old friends; they had talked for hours - about Ghana, their families, about life and many things. He had been enthralled by her explosive laughter, her irrepressible sense of humour and her childlike sense of wonder and naivete. He had told her about his pursuing a Masters degree in Economics and working to earn some pocket money. Coincidentally, she was also studying Economics as an undergraduate student in another university. It had been a God-given opportunity to assist her in her studies whilst deepening their friendship. Without hesitation, he had invited her to his apartment for dinner.

"It's the apartment of a philosopher." She had said as she had entered his apartment, noticing the various philosophical books on the bookshelf and posters hung up on his wall.

"I know." He had replied, flattered that she had noticed. "I love books."

She had been curious to find out all about him.

"Tell me one other thing I should know about you."

"I'm a frustrated bachelor looking for the right woman." He had looked at her intently, unable to hide his attraction to her. He remembered how she had lowered her eyes in embarrassment.

As he recalled the vivid images of the youthful days of friendship and pleasure, Adendo's thoughts poured out in breathless bursts:

I remember how we just held hands and walked through the park. And we would go out to the theatre and after that lurk around. I remember the times we would sit and look into each other's eyes till we were overcome by tender emotions. Sometimes, you would let me kiss you... And I loved you Serena! How I've often wondered the way things might have been between us if...if you had....

She had been no schemer for marriage, neither was she one who toyed with the affections of men. That was why it had been a shock to him when she had turned down his marriage proposal.

"Why?" He'd asked shocked.

"I am betrothed to another man. It is an arranged marriage. My parents expect it of me." She had said, visibly upset.

"What about us?" He'd held her, looking at her with pleading eyes.

"I have no choice." She had turned away, almost in tears. "The wedding has been planned."

"Why didn't you tell me? Why did you lead me on?" He had asked bitterly.

"I didn't mean to keep it away from you...I...I'd hoped....."

He had walked out on her, all his hopes...dashed.

After that devastating moment, they never spent time together - they never went out to eat a meal, watch a movie, go dancing, never phoned each other, never touched.....He would say that Tenkora stole from him what was rightly his.

What an irony that he had he received an invitation to join the Ghanaian trade Centre as the Commercial Director from nobody else but Serena's husband, Tenkora. It was without doubt an appointment based on Serena's recommendation. The guaranteed salary of a hundred million Cedis in addition to other allowances had enticed him.

Tenkora had taken him into his confidence from the moment they had begun working together.

"I have great plans for the Trade Centre. The application of advanced technology can develop agriculture and industry in Ghana beyond our wildest imagination."

He had been fascinated. From that time they had become close friends. Hence the need to consciously avoid Serena, not least because she was married but because she was married to one he liked well.

"It was your naivete Serena, you failed to realize that without love, sorry household realities would be too difficult to bear. It seems that fate is always teaching us new lessons." He whispered to himself sadly.

If any woman could love him, surely Serena could. There was such a wealth of love in her, and yet, she belonged to another man who didn't really want her. Perhaps Serena could leave Tenkora for him?

"No!" He swore at himself, appalled. Yet a part of him longed for this.

The full moon made deep shadows and the moonlight was upon his car, which moved like a white column in the shadowy dark. Down in North Ridge Street, where he lived, the evening light bland and calm, Adendo still felt menaced by disquieting memories. He drove slowly through the gates of his house with a heavy heart.

"Sweet illusion of my soul......." the romantic bolero rang. It was a song about love so far away that it hurt, of love so elusive that a woman could never know where she stood......

Serena sat cross-legged as she listened to the song, her face turned sideways and her cheek against the soft cushion. She stared at the luxurious souvenirs strewn all over the room. They were collections from the numerous countries to which her husband had attended conferences and reminders of her lonely nights.

She stopped short of her song. The word 'love' would lead her down a memory lane that was a deep and dangerous abyss. Yet it was an alluring impulse although self-destructive.

Like a strong magnet, her eyes were drawn to the large wedding picture of herself and her husband encased in a golden frame on the wall. Serena's eyes misted with emotion as she saw herself walking slowly through the bejeweled, gorgeously dressed guests, whispering gracious thank-yous to those who had heartily congratulated her. She had felt like a princess as many appreciative and admiring eyes had been fixed on her. Beneath her tranquil façade, her heat had raced in anticipation of what it would be like to be married to a handsome, successful and apparently romantic man, who had promised to love and cherish her.

Surprisingly, as she looked again at the picture, she noticed that his eyes looked icy cold. Had it been a vow of eternal hatred? She had been impressed by those eyes -intelligent, focused and set in a handsome face. He was a master negotiator, which had been the key to his undoubted success. He disarmed both friends and opponents with his compelling personality as he negotiated his way through life. His marriage to her now seemed to her like a negotiation – an act of cruel treachery.

The speed with which her marriage had deteriorated had been terrifying. It wasn't hate that had transformed the relationship – it was worse – utter indifference. They had struggled to live as best as they could in harmony and she has lost count of the number of anguished years of desolation. Yet it was a curious relationship. Tenkora loved to show her off to his friends – like a beautiful and rare art piece.

Her mind was thrown back to the first time she met Tenkora. He had looked charmingly handsome in his shiny black suit as he had waited to dance with her on that day. It had seemed magical when her father had whispered to her: "This is the man I would want you to marry."

Tenkora had whispered in her ears as she had danced in his arms: "Do you know what great things life has in store for you?"

"No" she had replied.

"My life is a beautiful journey with many dazzling dreams and I want to share it with you. Marry me and I will show you true love like no man ever could." He had told her.

Masterful and political, Tenkora had wormed his way into her heart with the apparently right words but she now realized that he had only been thinking about his dreams. She had been so hopeful that these passionate feelings would take firm roots and blossom in the ten years of their marriage. Yet she now realized that these words had not been representative of the thoughts that had lain in the depths of his mind.

She recalled how Tenkora had shamelessly lapped at the help and encouragement offered him by her father who was then the Head of the 'Agricultural Marketing Board' - several courses abroad, sponsored by the Board and finally a job as Manager for Research and Planning at the Ghanaian Trade Centre with recommendation from his patron. Now she was convinced that Tenkora only stayed married to her because of her father's properties.

Tenkora had been away for three days attending that conference in Nigeria, without even phoning her. She remembered the luxury of wonderful late-night phone calls with long, heart-revealing conversations she had once had with Adendo, who had once been her closest friend and confidant. She remembered the magic that had been created by being in the soft protective ambience of Adendo's love.

I had hoped to find with you Tenkora the emotional intimacy I once had with Adendo - the warm unselfish love, but after marriage I have realised that I was tricked. You played your enchanting role as a suitor very well but later revealed yourself to be a cold, vain and selfish man with no intention of giving me the joy and happiness you promised me. Now you write me this letter!

The thought of the letter sent chills down Serena's spine. What on earth had prompted him to write it?

CHAPTER 2

Tenkora felt extremely relieved when the two-day conference on the technological development in America ended. He was tired and hungry and eager to find Mr. Tortison and his associates, the Trade partners with whom he was going to sign the contract for the importation of farming machinery into his country. It was difficult to find them. Reporters were demanding statements, photographs were being taken, and delegates were discussing ideas on top of their voices.

Tenkora decided to take a walk round the Palm garden whilst he kept an eye out for him. The grounds of the Rembles Hotel looked inviting. The hotel was situated in the fabulous summits of the Juta hills in Nigeria. In the intense heat of the equatorial sun, overhanging fauna seemed to open their arms invitingly as their blades bristled with raindrops from a slight drizzle.

Ah! There he was - the ticket to his dreams! Tortison. He rushed up to him.

"Mr. Tortison?"

"Yes?"

"My name is Babanda, Tenkora Babanda, The Minister for Trade and Industry in Ghanaa."

"Oh Babanda!, very pleased to meet you. I gather you and I have some business to conduct."

"Certainly."

"Excellent. You must meet Mr. Rizo, my partner - a well-seasoned Nigeriaian businessman, who is also party to the contract. Rizo, come and meet our man."

Mr. Rizo walked over. Tenkora looked carefully at his lean features. Rizo was tall, lean and walked with a cock-sure swagger. He wore a leather jacket and gold rings, cufflinks, chains and bracelets. He had a mean smile and a cold, calculating look in his eyes made him appear foreboding.

"Ah, you are the Minister to sign the contract for the importation of the farming machines."

"Yes! Yes! I am."

"Why don't we find a place where we can find some measure of privacy? How about in a private room in the Hotel?"

Tortison nodded and gestured to Tenkora.

The three men made their way through the crowd to the hotel lobby to a private dining room. Mr. Tortison crossed his legs and relaxed into his chair.

"So you are the man who is the darling of farmers in Ghanaa." He drawled.

"Yes, that was the first success in my political ambition. I convinced the farmers to become more export oriented."

"At the right time too." Mr. Tortison interjected trying to prove that he had a lot of information on Tenkora."

"Right. Many hundreds of hectares growing cocoa were almost diversified into growing foodstuffs because of the tumbling cocoa prices. I convinced the President that the farmers needed support."

"You are indeed our man." Mr. Rizo said looking at Tenkora appraisingly. He proudly pulled out five or six sheets of paper and handed them over to Tenkora.

"This is a copy of the draft contract which I'm sure you must have studied thoroughly by now."

"Yes......."

Tenkora took his time, going through the document, studying it carefully. His sharp eyes suddenly caught sight of a clause - clause 27. There had been no clause 27. An alarm triggered deep within his brain.

"Clause 27 says that this contract will be signed on condition that you have the first refusal of the Ghanaian cocoa beans." Tenkora said puzzedly.

"We are talking trade here - a deal for a deal." Tortison's jaw hardened.

"There was no such clause in the draft."

"Well, let's say there's been a minor amendment."

"I'm sorry, I can't sign this contract. I'm answerable to the President."

"You know, there is a lot of money in it for you."

Mr. Tortison leaned across the table, looking straight at him. Tenkora was speechless. He was trying to buy him! The gall of the man! How dared he?

"We would expose your country to modern technology." Tortison continued." The benefits of our trade relationship will be far reaching for your people and this could make you a powerful man....."

Tenkora couldn't believe his ears.

"How can you expect me to sign this contract? This clause is prejudicial to our interests."

"Is it not a right position for us to sell you such useful farming machines? We are giving it to you at such a substantial discount and..."

"My country may need this farming technology," Tenkora cut in, "But we can only accept this on suitable terms, such as those previously agreed upon."

"How do you know what is good for your country? Your country is in a vicious cycle of poverty from which there is no escape except on our terms."

"Signing this contract is no solution."

"Think of all the money that you could have in your bank account." Mr. Rizo coaxed.

"Good God! I don't need that kind of money."

"I've known men like you before." Mr. Tortison said sardonically. "They start with only a little more ambition than most people but somewhere between one business deal and the next, they acquire a little taste for power. Then like a drug, they find themselves addicted. Power becomes a thrill they cannot live without."

"Speak for yourself!" Tenkora burst out, beginning to lose control.

"You'll learn." Mr. Rizo replied calmly.

"I'm sorry, I do not have the mandate to sign your contracts." Tenkora stated indignantly. "We are concerned with progressive economics not the manipulation of people like you."

"Do we sign these contracts?" Mr. Tortison extended his contract to Tenkora as he stood up. Tenkora looked at the hand, tendering him the document, without any gumption or show of guilt and he marvelled at the man's single-mindedness of purpose.

He did not accept it.

Tenkora walked pensively to the far end of the grand banquet hall where a grand reception was being thrown to entertain the conference participants. Nigeriaian culture - food, folk dances and music from indigenous musical instruments highlighted the event. Native decors such as Okujina patterns offered glimpses of the traditional way of life. The evening festivities also featured music from other American countries. Delicious dishes were being served with excellent wines.

Tenkora spotted one of the participants, Reverend Monis at a distance and decided to speak to him to find out more about the real man. He moved to where the Reverend was standing, savouring his drink.

"I would like to introduce myself. The name is Tenkora Babanda, Minister for Trade and Industry in Ghanaa."

"Well pleased to meet you Mr. Babanda. May we drink to the future prosperity of our beloved continent." He raised his glass.

"To our fame, power, wealth, in any order you like."

"I thought you had that already."

"What? With the standard of living in Ghanaa? Things are so hard nowadays my brother."

"True."

"Not even a good position in the government can buy you the essential commodities which are lacking."

"One can always shop abroad."

"How much can one carry?"

"I went to a shop abroad to buy a whole trolley of toiletries and the shop assistant looked at me as if I was from another planet. Are you going on an expedition? she asked."

Tenkora broke out in large guffaws of laughter and took a large gulp of beer.

"But there are some people who are able to profit from the misfortunes of their country." Reverend Monis added.

"That may not be a bad idea. Some leaders are idiots who will ruin everything if left to their own devices." Tenkora stated sardonically. Reverend Monis appeared shocked. "I'm just joking of course." He quickly added. "I'm at the moment just interested entering into profitable business deals on behalf of my country."

"Watch those you enter into business deals with at this conference." Reverend Monis warned. "There are some business men whose policy may be that of the Thug and the Prostitute."

"Really, What is that?"

"The prostitute will flatter their business partners but they do not necessarily mean what they say."

"And the thug?"

"The thug uses whatever weapon available in order to beat his victim into submission."

An icy cold feeling swept through Tenkora's body. The sound of cheers and clapping roused him from his dark thoughts. He turned to see a dancer in the middle of the dance floor, some distance from where he was standing.

The dancer was a joy to watch as he slid, bent, flailed his arms into various configurations, lilting forward, shaking his waist, and spreading his arms wider to embrace the world. His facial expressions added to the drama. Tenkora burst into joyous laughter, clapping excitely.

His smile was soon to wane however when the dancer began to sing a song with words that pierced deep into his heart.

"Don't cry, be a man, when your woman no give you what you want....."

Panic chords struck his brain, tearing lose his fears and cravings that had become for him a form of madness - his deep and passionate yearning for a child. He turned his back sharply to the dancer, anguish written all over his face, almost buckling over. His heart burned with bitter shame as his memory went back to the events that had led him to marry his wife Serena ten years ago:

Mr. Tiko's fiftieth birthday party had been the grandest party he had ever attended. It was at this party that he had experienced what was deeply buried in his nature - envy. It was not an envy of anyone in particular, but a suppressed antagonism towards people who had achieved the wealth and position he so much craved for. The fact that he had come from a family tradition of past glories lost forever rankled in his bitter thoughts. He had wanted to be as wealthy and powerful as Mr. Tiko.

He had found himself watching Serena from the crowd and had hardly touched what was in his plate as his eyes had closely followed her movements. With a ruthless singleness of purpose, he had suddenly desired Serena who had represented his ability to realize his dreams. At this moment, his envy had given way to the zeal to seize the opportunity for self-advancement.

He had found her stunningly beautiful, cultivated and intelligent. Her face had been arresting with dancing eyes set in an oval face with rounded cheeks and lovely dimples. Her evening gown had flowed enticingly from her hips. It had been easy to desire her.

She had been a sheltered child who had never known anything but simplicity and kindness. This made her loyal and kind - the very qualities he had been looking for in a wife. True, he had never stopped to wonder whether Serena was in love with him. He had been her father's choice, that had been what mattered and he had been successful enough to take care of her.

Now, Serena was utterly unlike the woman she had been when he had first seen her. She was to him like a faded flower - Barren! Unable to give him what he so much needed! A rage started welling up in him and he fought for control. He suddenly felt the urge to write to her another letter, to tell her to try another alternative – the village witch doctor. He could have some answers.......

Tenkora excused himself hastily and rushed into his hotel room to write what seemed to be the most important letters of his life – a second letter to Serena and another letter to explain

17

to the Board members of the Trade Centre why he did not sign the contract.

His pen flew quickly across the sheet as he sat at the desk. A vein pulsated at the side of his head as he poured out his thoughts on the paper. He ended his letters and sighed, drained of all energy. Looking for envelopes to seal, he groped under the desk for his briefcase.

Oh my God! In his anguish, he had left it behind in the banquet hall, where he had stood with Reverend Monis. He had to hurry to pick it up. There were some important documents inside, including his passport. He rushed to the Banquet hall and looked around the counter where he had been standing. The briefcase was not there. He was puzzled. Ah, perhaps, Reverend Monis had taken it up to his room for him.

Reverend Monis did not seem to have a clue about his briefcase when Tenkora called him. "Check at the reception desk." He suggested.

Tenkora rushed to the receptionist desk.

"Has anyone reported a missing briefcase?" He enquired.

"No." The lady at the desk shook her head.

Panic gripped him.

"Someone has stolen my briefcase. It is dark brown with gold clips." He announced, panting. "Call the police right away. It contains vital information. Very vital!"

"Are you sure, sir? Our security is very tight."

"Yes I am! I left it at the Banquet hall when I went there for the drinks."

"You have searched the hall thoroughly?"

"From top to bottom. Someone has stolen my briefcase. You must call the police." Tenkora's voice became sharp, urgent, excited.

"Alright, Mr. Babanda, we'll call in the police." The receptionist assured him. She walked over to another attendant at the counter who dialed a number. Tenkora wiped off the sweat from his forehead with an already wet handkerchief. He noticed that the receptionist looked alarmed at the message received over the phone.

"What is wrong?" Tenkora asked.

"Someone handed a dark brown executive briefcase with gold clips to the security. The owner of the briefcase is wanted for questioning."

A knot of anxiety formed in Tenkora's stomach. He saw two security men approaching. He didn't know what to think.

"You must come with us." One of them, wearing a green mufti with a khaki cap said abruptly as they reached him.

"Why?" Tenkora was astonished. "Where is my briefcase?"

"Please come!" The man again demanded. "We need you to answer some questions."

"What is all this about?" Tenkora was alarmed.

"You will soon find out." The security man escorted him towards an office within the Hotel.

A tall, bearded Nigeriaian official rose from behind the desk as they entered. The first thing that struck Tenkora was the presence of Mr. Tortison and Mr. Rizo. They were standing in the far corner of the room, discussing some documents.

"Good afternoon, Mr. Babanda. I am Mr. Mozo. Have a seat please." The man said curtly, gesturing to a chair opposite him. Tenkora sat down stiffly, studying Mr. Mozo apprehensively.

Mr. Mozo signaled the security man to bring to him a briefcase - Tenkora recognised it instantly as his briefcase.

"Th...That is my briefcase!" Tenkora shouted out. "What on earth are you doing with my briefcase?"

Mr. Mozo ignored him and opened it. He brought out some documents, studying them carefully.

"You have been found in possession of some illegal state documents." he said in a high-pitched voice.

"That is a lie." Tenkora protested, shocked. "Why would I be interested in illegal state documents? How could I even get access to them?"

Mr. Mozo watched Tenkora. His look was grim.

"You stole these documents." Mr. Mozo lifted documents. "They contain very highly confidential information of the state on a new technological innovation."

Tenkora was suddenly filled with anxiety. This was going too far. "No! I have never seen these documents in my life. This is a set up. I am only a Trade delegate.

Mr. Tortison can testify for me."

His denial seemed to infuriate Mr. Mozo the more.

"Silence!" he thundered, "Look, let me tell you something. The crime you have committed is punishable by several years in prison. Have you ever been in a Nigeriaian prison? Does your Ghanaian curiousity yearn to find out what our prisons are like? I can arrange that! Do you understand? I can arrange that!"

Tenkora shivered inwardly.

"Do you know this man?" Mr. Mozo, demanded from Mr. Tortison and Mr. Rizo. Tenkora saw them whispering amongst themselves. Mr. Tortison said smoothly. "I think you may have made a mistake. Could you please give us a few minutes with him to settle this matter? I will explain later."

Mr. Mozo got up and left the room.

"You shall be absolved of blame on only one condition." Mr. Rizo informed the dazed Tenkora in deceptively soft tones. "All it takes for this charge to be withdrawn is for you to sign the contract you earlier refused to sign. "

"What?" Said Tenkora, aghast.

"This is not too much to ask and is within your power. The other and only option is a number of years in the Nigeriaian prison and disgrace in your country."

Tenkora was speechless. No, he could not bear disgrace. He remembered...No, not disgrace. Somehow, he would find a way out of this.

His father's words suddenly came to him:

I tell you, law, order and respect humanity have flown out of the window. The world is collapsing into a crowd mentality, ruled by corruption and nobody cares. Nobody!

"I....I will sign the contract." He stammered, forcing the words out.

Mr. Rizo and Mr. Tortison smiled at each other. Mr. Tortison opened his briefcase and pulled out a document from it and handed it over to Tenkora with a golden pen.

"Read carefully and sign." Mr. Rizo stood over his shoulder smiling mercenarily.

Thoughts sped through Tenkora's mind as he signed the contract. He thought of his vision and ideals for agriculture in his country and his country's expectations of him. All those plans seemed to be dashed as he handed over control to strangers with one stroke of a golden pen.

One month later, a lady from work asked me to come and have a look at a litter of German Shepherd puppies that her mother-in-law had bred.

Considering that she was a registered breeder, I thought, 'Well, there's no harm in having a look.'

As we drove up the driveway of this very nice home on acreage, we were enthusiastically greeted by two stunning-looking dogs, one huge male and a long-coated female.

Once the human introductions were completed, we proceeded down the pathway to a shed near the stables. After poking my head through the door, I was speechless. There were eight gorgeous puppies all very eager to meet me. How could I possibly choose just one? I carefully sat down on the floor and was bombarded—licked everywhere possible, hair pulled, shoes chewed.Puppies played tug of war with my jeans and, as I sat there lapping up all this attention, my eyes focused on this one puppy who was just sitting back, ears forward, head slightly tilted, just watching all the frivolity happening around her. It was as if she were waiting for something.

After about fifteen minutes, the rest of the puppies began to settle down after wearing themselves out. Once the others had piled up for a nap, this one little girl calmly walked over, sat down beside me and gazed into my eyes.

When she placed one paw on my arm, my heart melted on the spot. Smart girl, almost as if she had it all planned. I no longer had to make that difficult choice; she had made that decision for me.

Now for that excruciating three week wait, both for myself as well as Casey, till I could bring her home.

Three weeks felt like an absolute lifetime, but I did manage to keep my mind occupied trying to think of names and buying all the usual puppy essentials, plus extras of course.

CHAPTER 3

The strike had been timed for the height of the harvest season. Almost magically, trucks that had been rumbling into the plantation had been suddenly stopped in their tracks. The farmers now stood with red bands tied around their heads and wrists, protesting aggressively.

Adendo stood on the large cocoa plantation in the Tano village, grimacing at the loud curses of the farmers as they unloaded the trucks. He felt as if this strike was a dagger aimed at his heart. The Tano was a large farming village situated at the southern end of the capital city with long-established role as a cocoa-farming village. It had a population of about nine thousand people, most of them farmers.

"We are going to lose money if the ships leave the port without all that cocoa." Adendo pleaded with the farmers.

"We are too hungry to tend the farms. We have not been paid what we have sold." The rising chorus of the farmers swelled.

"We will pay you for last month. We are just trying to gather up some money." Adendo tried to convince them as images of the depressing bank statement invaded his mind. "Please consider all that the Trade Centre has done for you. We have allocated government land to you at next to nothing."

"Yet still, we need to eat and pay our children's school fees." Atiemo, the chief farmer shouted, raising his fists in the air.

"Our Chief Executive has gone to Nigeria to bring some good news. Give us up to next week when he arrives and we will surely reward you."

Atiemo studied Adendo's sincere bearing and after some minutes reluctantly called his team of men together and addressed them. They appeared temporarily pacified and began reloading the trucks, mumbling unhappily to themselves.

Adendo felt relieved as he watched the trucks leave for the city. He hated to see anything go to waste. His own ambition in life had been borne out of outrage at his father's waste of financial, physical and mental resources. From a rich cocoa farmer, his father had fallen into poverty through financial mismanagement. As a result, he Adendo had taken a policy of making decisions quickly and acting decisively - never second-guessing himself.

Mr. Egare, Dr. Ragu and Mrs. Azuri, Board members of the Trade Centre were waiting for some feedback from him in the Board-room as he returned to the office.

"Has Tenkora signed the contract yet?" Mr. Egare asked. Mr. Egare, the National chief farmer was a highly ambitious man. His exuberant disposition and round solid build formed a combination to be found in prosperous traders.

"I haven't heard anything but I'm sure he'll do the job." Adendo lied. He had decided not to reveal to the board members the contents of Tenkora's letter, in which he had declared that he would not sign the contract.

"Tenkora was not the man to send to Nigeria to sign that contract. We should have sent Mrs. Azuri who is the lawyer." Dr. Ragu stated with none of his usual suaveness. Dr. Ragu was a renowned economist and a consultant to the Trade Centre. He had struggled several years and had expected to be chosen as the Chairman of the Trade Centre but Tenkora was taken. He hid his bitterness well with his assured air and ease of manner.

"Mr. Egare shifted uneasily in his seat. He was from the same tribal group as Tenkora and felt the need to defend him. Tenkora had also been responsible for all the large contracts he received from the Trade Centre to supply seedlings and fertilizer.

"Tenkora is a man of sound judgement and the best man to have signed that contract." He insisted.

"Dr. Ragu made a rude noise. "The fact that the country educates a human being abroad to become some stupid bureaucrat with a big job and handsome salary does not mean he is the right person to represent his people for every trade deal!"

"Well I must say that it may take a lawyer to bargain for influence when it comes to certain sticky parts of a contract." Mrs. Azuri added. Mrs. Azuri was a lawyer and legal advisor to the Trade Centre, a lady with a good head and sharp eyes. She had been well educated, both locally and abroad. She was however a highly-strung woman, who often felt unfairly treated because she was female.

"You are not showing as much commitment to the Chairman as is expected of you." Mr. Egare retorted harshly.

"How......how dare you!" Mrs. Azuri gasped, angered. "How dare you question my loyalty."

"I realize that some people are more worthy of position than others and I am going to suggest this to the Chairman. Mind you, this has nothing to do with sexism." Mr. Egare continued.

Mrs. Azuri was incensed. "I am aware of the fact that you are an ambitious man, seeking power, position and prestige."

"What about you?" He sneered. "Your loyalty must be to the Chairman to whom you owe your bank account, your name, your position!"

"Mr. Egare, that is uncalled for!" Adendo cut in firmly.

Mrs. Azuri, now obviously very angry, got up to leave the conference room.

"Mrs. Azuri! Please don't leave." Adendo said, trying to stop her.

"Let her go. I know her type of woman - clothes and jewels, with primary interest in herself. Social butterfly, just good for cocktails and parties." Mr. Egare sneered.

"Mr. Egare, that is enough!" Adendo warned. Adendo's tone had become very dry indeed. He felt very embarrassed by the unpleasant situation. He could hardly wait for Tenkora to return from his trip to explain himself.

....

Alima, Personal Assistant of Tenkora, sat listlessly at the airport, waiting for her boss to arrive from the conference in Nigeria. Turbulent thoughts had been raging in her head all morning. Alcohol alone, she thought, would give her the composure that she needed.

Tenkora represented so much to her. He was her stepping-stone to all the things she had ever wanted in life but couldn't have. Life had never been so good since she had begun working for Tenkora – a sweet combination of business and pleasure. Lavish compliments, passion-filled kisses and expensive gifts along with a fat salary were more than she had bargained for. Now, her whole family looked up to her. They were poor but would not be for long if she attained her dream of being his wife. The appeal of his throng of rich friends and admirers, the dazzle of their lifestyle and the breathtaking display of wealth convinced her that she had to become his wife.

That isn't asking too much, is it? No, this is just urban survival!

Subtle moves were not driving home the message, so now she had to resort to bold moves. She had once overheard a heated argument he had had with his wife. He had been shouting certain recriminations at her. That stuck up bitch couldn't give him any children. Oh yes, she smiled to herself. She had her ways and means to get him.

....

The plane landed at Ghanaian airport in Tendam exactly at 7.00 p.m. on the Friday evening. It was with slow, deliberately seductive steps that Alima approached Tenkora as he walked through Immigration.

"I must appear as seductive as I can, to catch his undivided attention. I feel as good as I look in my short red skirt, tight red blouse with a low cut neckline and lofty high heels. Oh there he is! I must flash him my most winning smile."

"Tenkora!" She squealed in delight as she threw her arms around his neck. Her artificial hair fanned like a cushion on his chest. He cradled her softness against his chest and slid his hands up the sides of her neck until he cupped her face in his fingers, their eyes meeting. Lost in admiration, Tenkora was brought to himself by the sight of his wife and Adendo approaching.

Adendo watched the embrace with his mouth pursed tightly in disapproval. Tenkora looked up, gently pushing Alima aside. Serena's eyes as she registering the scene with shock confronted him. Tenkora swallowed nervously.

"Hello, Tenkora." Serena said coldly. Her usual soft and smooth voice betrayed a typical unsteadiness. She fiddled with the gold ring on her right index finger as she stood before her husband and Alima.

"Serena, how are you?" Tenkora looked at her uneasily.

Serena struggled for control "Fine. How are you?" She replied.

Alima looked at Serena. She saw good skin and long, lovely hair, nicely styled, well cut suit. How beautiful and classy she was! A sharp pang of envy stung Alima and she shook hands reluctantly. She felt a sudden urge to sway the confidence of Serena.

"Good to see you back home." Adendo forced out.

"Thank you Adendo. I....." Tenkora's voice trailed off before his accusing eyes.

Any letter or important correspondence?" He turned to Alima.

Triumphantly, Alima moved closer to Tenkora. "There are two letter marked 'Very urgent' and an important call from the President regarding them." She handed over the letters.

Adendo held tightly on to Serena's hands, the expression on his face stunned and uncomprehending.

"Let me see whether I have got this right or whether I am just imagining it, Tenkora is having an affair with Alima!" The unsavoury realisation dawned on him and gnawed at his heart. "How could he compare somone like Alima to Serena?"

"Adendo, could you please see Alima home. And let's have dinner tomorrow okay?" Tenkora said with a straight face.

Adendo opened the door of his black Mercedes Benz and Alima slid into the passenger side behind him. Alima closed her eyes and inhaled the odour of the expensive leather interior, leaning further into her seat. Adendo looked displeasingly at her.

"In order to gain our own ends, it is easy to be indifferent to other people's feelings." He stated quietly, his words heavy with accusation.

Alima eyed him defiantly.

"You amaze me, Alima. Is that the best you could do, going for another woman's husband? And that man happens to be your boss?"

"Tenkora and I have a father-daughter relationship."

"You are a hypocrite and a liar!"

"You have no right to call me names. I could tell Tenkora about this and..."

"Look, get out of my car!" Adendo shouted, his patience reaching its limits with Alima. He stopped at the side of the road to enable her get out of the car. Alima banged the car door and walked off in a huff.

"How could you jeopardise your marriage by having an affair with such an imp Tenkora." Adendo shook his head in disbelief.

Tenkora looked guiltily at Serena as they drove home in their chauffeured driven Mercedes Benz. Serena stared out of the window as if unaware of her husband's presence. Worry dampened her previous anticipation. Her face was masked in tears. Tenkora, frowning, looked at her questioningly and got a stony glance in return. He sat back with his arms folded defensively.

Stars hung poised in the darkness. It was a full moon night. Oppressed by rising hopelessness and feeling fate's malevolent touch, Serena missed the beauty of the night.

CHAPTER 4

At the residence of Tenkora Babanda, a blast of heavy sound greeted the guests. Adendo found a stool at the wine bar at the far end of the room and drank a glass of wine, whilst observing the party. Serena walked towards him. How alluring she looked! She wore a distinctive blue velvety gown with a low-cut neckline and pearls to grace her neck. She had her hair parted in the middle, which accentuated her full red lips, giving her a sensuous look. Their eyes held. Feeling a torrent of response, he was unable to withhold the emotions revealed unexpectedly in him.

"Oh Serena, how are you?" He asked as she walked up to him

"Fine, thank you Adendo and you?'

"Oh, I'm well."

Adendo was rescued from a stifling silence by the presence of Serena's Aunt, Aunt Tami. Aunt Tami was a large, big-bosomed woman with stunning facial beauty that had been marked by the hardships of life. Nevertheless, her sophistication and her vibrant gestures, made her a very attractive personality. She smiled at Adendo and put her hands through Serena's arms and gave her a slight tug. "Come child, I need to talk to you."

"Look Serena, why don't you leave him? That man does not deserve you." Auntie Tami showed great impatience for what she thought was Serena's 'trapped life'.

"Auntie, our problems are mainly because we can't have children."

"You mean he can't have children. Remember what the doctor said – you are all right."

"But Auntie – "

"Look Serena, if it is children that he wants, you will have children. After all, it is only a woman who knows the father of her child."

Serena shook her head and pulled Aunt Tami to the corner to continue their conversation.

....

The cocktail became more alive as excited chatter filled the room. People indulged themselves, gulping down beer and tucking in savoury meats. The live band spilled out loud highlife music and bodies began to respond to the music. Adendo could see Tenkora in a tight corner with Alima on the dance floor. She was whispering sweet nothings in his ear.

It was not sweet nothings that Alima was whispering into Tenkora's ear.

"Marry me." She was saying.

Tenkora was silent. The shock stopped his breath in earnest for a moment, cursing himself for not seeing where she was heading. Then he said, his mouth against her hair. "Darling, at the right time....Please understand."

Her movement was like that of a great snake as she snuggled further in his arms, her arms sliding smoothly around his neck. She was all over him, and against him.Her breath came in short, sharp snorts under her nostrils and she made small grunts like an animal. Tenkora fought for control but couldn't find it.

Mr. Egare who whispered something into his ear rescued him just in time. Tenkora nodded and thankfully took the wineglass being handed to him, turning to the crowd.

"To the success of Tenkora's trip!" Mr. Egare proposed a toast.

"To the success of his trip." The guest replied, raising their glass. Stakeholders gathered around Tenkora to question him how he managed to seal the deal when his letter gave such a different impression.

"Was there some initial disagreement before you signed the contract?"

"Could I sit and watch Ghanaa drown? I had to take a bit of a risk initially though."

"What did you do?"

"I twisted their arm to give us a better price, which they refused at first, of course."

"In your letter, you called them 'thug' and 'prostitute'. Were they underhand in any way?"

"Well, I thought so in the beginning when they suggested an increase in price as a result of the re-negotiation in the payment terms."

"So you managed to get them to beat down the price?"

"I am accustomed to handling tricky affairs of state and when matters have reached a deadlock, I explore avenues and take prompt steps through the proper channels."

Tenkora smiled, feeling very proud of himself as he walked around the hall. When all questions seemed exhausted, he perched beside the wine bar.

"It's great to have a devoted wife." Adendo's said quietly behind Tenkora, causing him to turn suddenly around to face him.

"I am not going to remind you of that, Adendo." Tenkora replied patting him on the shoulder.

"Serena is one of the most beautiful, talented, kind and devoted women I have ever encountered in my life. You are blessed to have a wife like that. Now, don't throw it all away, do you hear me?"

"Throw it away? Why would I?"

"It seems to me that you have taken her for granted."

"I am a very busy man, Adendo. I have been busy providing for her and all those other relatives who depend on me."

"No, you are too busy paying attention to the wrong people."

Tenkora folded his arms defensively. "When you were married, were you never attracted to anybody apart from your wife?"

"That is no excuse. I must give you a very solemn warning against having an affair with Alima. Women like her like to fall in love with handsome rich men like you. They begin their campaign with flattering advances and make a quick conquest by binding you to them with unbreakable fetters of lust. My friend, it is okay to let a little wine go into your head but don't let it get to your thighs!"

"But Adendo, put yourself in my shoes." Tenkora stated pensively. "Imagine that Adelina had been an affectionate, gentle woman, who was ready to give you everything you asked for but could not give you that one thing which you so much desired...."

"What is that?"

"A child."

"I would have......" Adendo began, embarrassed.

"Could you possible cast her off or does one take pity on her, marry another woman and then make amends?"

"Well, you must excuse me there." Adendo wagged his finger protestingly. "You know I separate women into two categories. Adelina was a spider, Serena is...."

"Not giving me a child." Tenkora interrupted. "Denying facts is no answer. What is to be done? Tell me. I am full of life and I feel I can longer love my wife, however much I esteem her because she cannot give me a child. How am I to act in such a conflict? It is not my intention to hurt her."

"If you want my opinion, when you have a loving and faithful wife and you love her, there is no conflict. Children may be important but there are ways and means....."

"True, but I want legitimate children."

"I wasn't even talking about that. How about adoption? You've adopted Ayisi, haven't you? I mean, Serena is such a loving wife..." Adendo broke off suddenly realised he was getting overly emotional.

"Well, enough, enough. I do not think your own marital record entitles you to give advice - "

Suddenly alerted by the sound of the crash in the study room, Tenkora stopped short and then walked quickly towards the room, followed by Adendo.

Alima recoiled from their shocked gaze with a guilty expression. Auntie Tami was moaning loudly and clutching her eye.

"She called me a prostitute!" Alima said defensively.

"And that is exactly what you are. How dare you assault my Aunt in my own house." Serena shouted at her. Locked to the gaze of murderous eyes, she did not see Alima's fist close over a flower vase and raise her hands, braced for impact.

Adendo threw himself between Alima and Serena. "Alima, put that away at once!" Adendo demanded furiously. Alima ignored the command and threw her weapon, aiming at Serena's face. Serena dodged and over-balanced, tumbling backward. Adendo lurched towards her and tried to catch her before she fell. He caught her left-handed as she tottered and spun his own body with unbridled strength, managing to cushion her fall. The hard edge of the table dug into his ribs. Gratified to see her opponent in pain, Alima made an attempt to leave the room. A strong hand restrained her by grabbing her upper arm and pulling her back into the room.

"You are not leaving this room until you apologise to my wife and her aunt"

"Why should I?" Alima replied unabashed. "She called me a prostitute."

Tenkora wished the floor would swallow him up. This was the last thing he had expected to happen in his house.

"Why?" Adendo asked. "Did you sleep with her husband?" His biting question allowed no grace for reply.

"That is no business of yours!" Alima's words had a ringing arrogance.

"What did you say?" Adendo demanded, looking at her murderously.

She folded her arms defensively.

A warning not spoken in words, hung in Tenkora's eyes as he struggled to find the right words to rebuke Alima. She walked off unapologetically.

With Serena's body against his chest, Adendo leaned forward to ease his bruised side. Serena collapsed against his shoulder, weeping. Tenkora looked on as Adendo hugged Serena tightly, unable to hide his disapproval. Recognition suddenly caused Adendo to release Serena suddenly as if her body burned.

Tenkora's eyes explored the face of Auntie Tami - there were no cuts, only inflamed skin - a small enough penalty for causing him so much embarrassment.

Adendo gathered his scattered composure. Straightening his shirt, he walked out of the room without a word. Auntie Tami stormed after him.

Tenkora sucked in a ragged breath. He walked to the window and for a long time he stood staring out of it.

The tears came so fast to Serena's eyes that the damp sleeves of her dress no longer served to dry them. She leaned on the table and thrust her face, steaming and wet into the bend of her arm and went on crying, not caring to dry her face, her eyes, her arms.

"I'm sorry." Tenkora said, trying to calm her down. "I'm sorry." he repeated several times. The insincerity of his words struck Serena as she studied his expression. She looked long and hard at Him. Her look spoke of many, many recriminations.

Now don't go throwing it all away, do you hear me? Adendo's words rang in Tenkora's ears. It was not that he wanted to lose Serena. She could not give him children and he felt he had earned the right to have a girlfriend. He was also coming slowly to the conclusion that Alima, while not exactly indispensable to him, was perhaps, irreplaceable. She had just the right feminine combination of familiarity and respect; she made him feel important without letting him feel he was pompous. She was interested in his money of course, but wouldn't there have been something wrong with a woman of her age and situation if she wasn't?

....

I do not think your own marital record entitles you to give advice. Tenkora's words came back to Adendo as he settled down to sleep. Ancient images were summoned, unsettling memories, the bitter past. It had left behind deep, rampaging hurt that left unhealed wounds in its wake. Sometimes the anguish sliced into him with enough force and cruelty to make him want to weep. But he had leant from his childhood that men did not weep. The memory of his marriage to his ex-wife, Adelina was thrust on him. He grimaced as he recalled the dramatic way in which she had left him after the tragic death of their six-year old son.

Adelina, a white lady from a middle-class home in Bendon, had found it difficult to adapt to the frustrations of life in a developing country.

" I want us to build a life here for Terry." He had always coaxed her. "The future will be bright for him here."

Adendo now realised that Terry was the reason why she had stayed and after Terry died, there was no argument to hold her. Caught up and twisted in their nightmare, they could no longer find comfort in each other. A gnawing silence had risen like a monster between them.

"Why should it have been Terry? He was so gay and mischievous, always ready to laugh and we loved him. He was playing and shouting, and a few months later, he was gone forever. Oh why didn't he survive the cancer." Tears stung his eyes as resentment tore at his heart.

He suddenly felt a sudden need to have Serena close to him, so that they could cry in each other's arms and erase the pain of their past. After a brief hesitation, he decided to call her on her mobile phone, which he had kept written in his diary but had never used.

"Hi." Serena's sweet voice sounded like music to his ears.

"Hello. I was just ringing you to find out how you were feeling. I'm sorry for what happened tonight."

"Oh don't be sorry it was not your fault."

"I'm sorry because Serena, you don't deserve this. You are such a wonderful person."

"Oh you are so nice…."

Nice, Adendo mused. Words like this from Serena's lips sounded gentle and tender and special.

"Serena, I want you to know that I will always be there for you and that I believe in you like I've always done."

"Thank you so much Adendo." Serena whispered "I am very grateful."

There was a sudden awkward silence.

"Goodnight." Adendo whispered.

He almost switched off his phone until he heard Tenkora and Serena exchanging harsh words in the background:

"You have been receiving clandestine calls from Adendo?" Tenkora was asking in a harsh voice.

"He was worried about me." Serena was stating indignantly. "Adendo is an old friend."

"How old and how close a friend?" Tenkora was asking. "Why does he not mind his own business and find himself another wife. Any arguments in my house does not concern him!" Tenkora was raging on.

The phone rang off. Adendo wished he had heard some more. He shook his head almost felling ashamed at himself.

"You can't hide love", he admitted to himself. "But I would always be loyal to Tenkora, who is my friend."

....

In the bedroom of Tenkora and Serena they argued on after Serena turned her back to place her mobile phone on the bedside table.

Serena's heart began to pound as she imagined Adendo may have heard some of the conversation. She turned to Tenkora: "Goodnight" she stated silently.

Tenkora narrowed his eyes dangerously. "I remember it was you who recommended him for the job but I did not know that the two of you were this close…."

"No, No." Serena quickly tried to dispel any suspicious thought in Tenkora's mind. "He was just an old school mate, almost like a brother."

"Well, then if he was like a brother he would have by now advised you to produce a child for you husband to save your marriage."

"I have tried – "

"You? I have tried! Did I even not write to you from Nigeria to tell you to visit the marabout who was recommended to us, to see whether he could help?"

"Tenkora, I have seen over thirty doctors and tried insemination three times! I am so tired!" Serena burst into tears as she wrenched her desperation from her heart.

Tenkora looked at her, suddenly filled with dark and treacherous emotions that swirled within him. Without even a gesture of gentle persuasion, he threw himself on her and crushed her body to the bed, violently trampling on al the gentler emotions of her heart.

"You have very few chances to give me my child!" he growled under his breath.

Sernea's body was numb and Tenkora could not fell the softness of her warmth as she lay frigid in his arms. Warmth and softness now seemed far beyond his reach as he forcefully took what was his, wrenching out from her what she was yet to give to him.

Serena lay empty as deep ominous voices shouted at her, as her husband lay exhausted, sleeping by her side.

"It is only a mother who knows the father of her child." Auntie Tami's words haunted her as she struggled with her dark thoughts. Her mental struggles continued into a dream:

She is making her way through a forest searching for something. The forest is large and exceptionally beautiful. As she searches, she finds herself first moving up one tiny path that becomes blocked and then another, till she feels totally lost and bewildered, unable to decide how to proceed. Then suddenly two children appear, take her hand and lead her towards a man who stretches out his arms. It is not Tenkora! Just as she is about to identify who the man is, she wakes up.

CHAPTER 5

The acclaim won from the media by Tenkora for signing the contract for the importation of farming machinery was flattering:

"The golden moment to turn the fate of agriculture in Ghanaa around belonged to Tenkora Babanda as he signed the contract for the importation of farming machinery at the American Trade Conference. Tenkora Babanda is the new blood, who could reinvigorate the agricultural industry and take it to the next level."

Tenkora felt very pleased with himself as he read the newspapers with pride. Being cornered by Tortison and Rizo had not been a bad thing after all, he thought to himself. Now, not only was he famous, he was also rich. Tortison had placed a cool two million dollars in his account, with promise of another million dollars when they had made sufficient profit from the cocoa beans trade. What was thought to be sufficient could be another matter all together but Tenkora did not care. He was on the way to realizing his dreams.

He reflected on his game plan carefully. The introduction of the farming machinery, which were to arrive at the port the following week had to be successful. That would earn him an irrefutable reputation. But it would be a hard and arduous task. Who could be he rely on? Adendo of course!

He knew beyond doubt that Adendo inspire the speed and energy needed to distribute the machinery and get the farmers using the equipments. However, he had to be careful that Adendo did not try to steal the limelight from him.

Adendo has begun to speak out his mind against me. He had the guts to tell me how to treat my wife. He has never done that before. Can I still trust him? Could it be that he has feelings for Serena that I never knew. I don't like the way he held her at the party. Is he trying to compete with me for what I have?

Tenkora decided not to let his suspicion of Adendo interfere with their relationship at this time when he needed him. He was going to use him but watch him carefully. And of course, Adendo never needed to know about his deals with Tortison and Rizo. Tenkora was quite sure there would be many more. He had officially invited Tortison and Rizo over to Ghanaa to introduce them as key investors of the Trade Centre and they were arriving the next day.

....

Both Tenkora and Adendo had made predictions about their new project and both had turned out to be wrong or, in Adendo's case, half wrong. Adendo had been wrong, even if slightly to assume the farmers will willingly join the farmer's union for easy access to the new farming machinery. The farmers did not believe that the Trade Centre had any other aim than to squeeze all they could out of them and did not want to adopt any new farming methods. They just wanted higher prices for their farm produce. Organized labour was flexing its muscles and doing it cleverly. There was fever in the air and most of the farmers were now infected. Leaders of the farmers' union had spread the voice of dissatisfaction and the contagion was catching on fast. Adendo made efforts to convince the farmers that most of their fears were based on rumours and that the

Trade Centre was organising a surprise package for them. But even the disclaimer did not seem to reduce the impatience of the farmers.

"The Trade Centre is offering you agricultural equipment for deep ploughing, planting and harvesting." Adendo addressed the discontent farmers on the Koko plains, one of the largest farmlands registered with the Trade Centre. "I believe in people standing on their own two feet."

"What is the use of all these machines to us poor people."

"We are not going to give you free fish but instead we are going to teach you how to fish. It is about self-help. We will be giving out machinery that would make your work easier at highly subsidised prices. Then later, we will offer you interest-free loans to expand your farms.

"All we want is our daily bread and the perpetuation of our lineage and culture." Timo, a chief farmer who was known to have vast amounts of land protested.

"You are intelligent people, with a culture of many centuries. But what is your future? There is the need for all of us to be as industrious as ants."

"You are suggesting that without your help our civilisation will fall apart. Do you think we are wasting here in this village?" Adonu, another influential farmer asked indignantly.

"What other way is there?" Adendo asked, looking at him closely.

"Well, I'm not going to allow it to happen. I'll stop the whole thing from happening." Adonu pointed his finger rudely at Adendo.

Adendo looked hard at him. "You look at me and you see an enemy. You are therefore becoming fearful. All I want is that we help each other ....."

"Then pay us more money to take care of our families."

"If together, we should form a farmer's union, we can reduce costs, improve product quality, provide education to increase agricultural production. Your incomes would go up and your quality of life will be enhanced."

It had been like a miracle when after hours of persuasion the farmers unanimously agreed to accept the farming machinery.

Adendo stood on the farm with the 'Triple Performer' in hand and tried to demonstrate its use. It was an all-purpose cultivator that could perform three different functions – tollage of large acres, seedbed preparation and planting. The farmers watched fascinated as Adendo unfolded the compact machine and adjusted the depth and angle. "You see, you just allow the power of the machine to take control." He explained as he applied it to the pineapple farm, cutting down several pineapples at a time.

When he realized that the farmers were impressed, Adendo went to the truck and picked up several machines, handing them over to them to try it.. The farmers worked slowly at first as they got accustomed to the machines. Soon, they were working without stopping or showing the slightest sign of fatigue. The pineapples cut with a juicy sound and fell in fragrant rows. Despite the intense heat of the sun, the harvesting did not seem such hard work as the powerful machinery gave vigour and energy to their labour.

After three hours of hard work, Adendo looked around him and hardly recognised the farm. Everything was so altered. All the pineapples lay neatly cut in rows and the thick foliage that accompanied it were lying in heaps around them. With obstructions out of the way, the water from the furrows gleamed. Adendo suddenly realised how much work had been done that day. Forty men had finished the harvesting which previously took a hundred men to finish in three days!

....

"I would like to introduce to you our two consultants for the farming machinery project, Mr. Rizo and Mr. Tortison. They are also the consultants for the Cocoa Processing Project which we intend to implement by next year."

Tenkora leaned back in his chair as he tried to explain the new position to the board members of the Trade Centre. "Now, my friends, fortune smiles on us, and the path to real national greatness is open to us."

Adendo was not impressed with the bearing of Tortison and Rizo. There was a defiance, a restlessness about Rizo's face that made him uneasy. The stubborn set of Tortison's jaw also seemed to suggest that he would go to any lengths to further his ambitions.

"So how do you intend to raise the funds?" He asked.

"Well," Tortison cleared his throat. "We intend to raise part of the funds from local investors and part from a leasing company in Meriga."

"These are seasoned business men you know." Tenkora declared proudly.

"Well, we need to be certain that their experience and skills combine to make such a venture failure-proof."

It couldn't be Adendo who spoke in reply. Tenkora reflected. Adendo had never opposed any of his ideas.

"Call us financial wizards." Rizo replied.

Adendo caught Tenkora's look and decided to keep quiet although an ominous inner voice rang loudly in his ears, expressing concern. He decided to excuse himself from the trip to the site of the intended cocoa processing factory. Everything seemed to be going too fast!

Ahead, the road narrowed and bent sharply around the jugged hill that led to the Afiram plains. The land rover bounced over several large rocks and slowly proceeded through the curve. Tenkora was not perturbed. Below the rocks rose massive plains of rich, fertile land and his heart swelled with pride as he neared it. A large proportion of this cultivated land belonged to his father-in-law who was soon to bequeath it to his only daughter. He felt as if he owned this place already. This treasure was the reason why he would never divorce Serena.

"This is a great site for the cocoa processing factory. There are large cocoa farms here." He addressed Tortison.

Tortison did not reply. He was busy staring out of the window at the large plantation that lay ahead of them. It was a delightful plantation brimming with colors; red, green and orange from the blossoms of the farm produce. The well-cultivated land led through green fields, among mango groves, guava trees, pawpaw, mango, pineapples and pear trees. On both sides of the land, stretching as far as the eye could see were green, cultivated fields of cocoa with wide patches of plantain and other tubers. The rivers were wide here, almost a mile and very deep; in the mid-stream, they were clear and blue.

"This plantation belongs to my father-in-law." Tenkora boasted.

"Can we meet him?" Tortison asked.

"He is very old. My wife and I are due to inherit it soon."

"Wow!" Rizo exclaimed, fascinated at the size of the land.

"At the very end is an ideal spot for the cocoa-processing factory." Tenkora pointed out to the horizon.

"This farm is incredibly beautiful." Mr. Tortison said as he got out of the vehicle, completely ignoring Sessou. The air was refreshing and he took in several deep breaths.

A woman, followed by an elderly man approached them, carrying a basket and walking with rhythmic grace. Tenkora recognized the woman as Tiko, the Queen mother's daughter and the older man was Roku, one of the elders in the Chief's palace. Tiko smiled invitingly as she held out her basket which was filled with pawpaw.

"Welcome sir, have some ripe pawpaw. Ripe pawpaw is food for travelers. It is cool and satisfying."

"Thank you madam." Mr. Rizo picked one of the pawpaw which she had peeled and sliced, looking very impressed. The fruit tasted delicious.

She smiled and walked off laughing merrily. Mr. Rizo watched her as she swung her hips rhythmically. "I think I can do good business here." he enthused.

"The Chief is now ready to see you. Come with me."

They saw the chief and his elders communing when they entered the palace grounds. Chief Attito was a large man, very dark and powerfully built. Tortison wondered if the chief worked out or carried weights. He wore a white silk mantle with a red silk cord over his shoulder suspending three sapphires encased in gold. Round his neck hung heavy gold-plait necklaces of the most intricate artistry and his fingers were clustered with heavy gold rings. His bracelets were the richest mixture of beads and gold. He was seated in a low chair, richly ornamented with gold. He wore sandals of green, red and white leather.

"Greetings Nana." Tenkora said upon entering. "Greetings Nana." The others repeated.

The chief nodded. His head was held high with authority and he sat very still. Yet in spite of his stillness, he seemed thoroughly aware of every movement around him.

Rizo reeled at the sight of so much gold. Greed raged through his mind about how much wealth they could make from such a richly endowed village. He could not speak the local dialect. He crossed his, fingers depending on Tenkora to be an effective spokesman.

Chief Attito nodded at his linguist who addressed Tenkora and his team in a loud voice. "What is your mission here, you and your friends?". Tenkora stood up and nodded politely at all the elders in the room as was the custom. He addressed the elders in the local dialect:

"Chief Attito, I have come here to introduce these business men. We want to build a Cocoa Processing factory in this village to process all the cocoa."

They sat quietly. "How will this benefit the village?" The linguist asked after consultation with the Chief.

"Processing the cocoa means we will be able to sell the cocoa at higher prices and your village will become rich."

One of the elders, Sigoru, got up to speak. He was a large, aggressive man, full of vigor and known in the village to be very strong since he had killed a tiger with his bare hands. The tone of his voice was sharp and excited and an aggressive look crept into his eyes as he spoke.

"You call these people 'Business friends'. From what I know, business and friendship do not go together. Many people who end up doing business in the village offer nothing to the villagers on whose shoulders they are standing. They are coming to take our land. That's the key - money."

"No white man is interested in helping this village." Another elder, Sessou said aloud to Tortison's hearing.

"How do you know that?" Tenkora enquired.

Sessou looked at him with piercing eyes, suddenly angry. "I know! Some of our ancestors were sold as slaves."

"We must forget the past." Tenkora was impatient. "We must move on."

Sessou turned to look straight in the eyes of Tenkora.

"You see this scar," he pointed to his face. "I could have avoided the fight with the white man. I could have kept away from his woman but for a burning anger inside me." He hit at his chest dramatically.

Tenkora looked at him with new seriousness. "These people are from Nigeria and Rizo is a black man like you and me."

"Clever black man." Sessou sneered.

"It's a straight deal – we want to make this village rich."

"Yeah, that's in the Bible." Sessou retorted sarcastically.

Chief Attito thrust up his head in an authoritative gesture. "I do not want to sound ungrateful. However, I am here to preserve the traditions. We need money for basic necessities. We do not want to sweat ourselves to make others rich. If you have anything else to say which is about instant cash we will listen."

Tenkora quickly removed a large packet from his bag, containing five hundred thousand cedis. He handed it to the linguist. "This is for the renovations of the palace. We are here to prove to you how much we can transform this village and put money in the pocket of your sons."

The chief seemed pleased with this gesture and his expression softened. He whispered into the linguist's ears.

"Give us some time. We will have a meeting tonight to

Tenkora was pleased at these words and left the palace happily with his team.

....

Tenkora finally managed to convince Rizo and Tortison to stay overnight at his small guesthouse in the village and enjoy the night entertainment. Tortison wondered how an educated man clad in a western suit in a modern office in the city during the week could return to the village over the weekend to immerse himself in tribal festivities in a traditional manner. He didn't wonder for long as he stood mesmerised watching the 'Mapuka' dance. The drums were beating out gay rhythms. The spectacle was fascinating, exotic. The men beating the drums were concentrated as they beat the insistent rhythm. It was a fascinating dance with powerful and sensuous body movements. The dancer's body quivered to the rhythm of the drum as she twisted her waist, which appeared as flexible as a rubber band, and thrust her backside back and forth invitingly or so it appeared to Tortison who stood mesmerised, intoxicated by the dance.

His gaze dropped to the dancer's rounded breast that was half exposed in a tight scanty bikini, swathed with colourful beads. It followed the line of her bared back, adorned with colourful paint marks, down to the tantalizing mould of flesh exposed to his view beneath the loincloth. Her body glistened with sweat. It was beautiful, well formed, slender and supple. This was a body that was created for a man's hands.

Tortison couldn't get his mind off the lady who had danced the 'Mapuka' dance. He felt like a man bewitched. He stopped, lit a match and threw it in the waters and walked aimlessly, hovering around the bush, as if to see his if 'Mapuka' lady would appear. The evening light was on the water, and the dark trees were against the setting sun. The misty droplets on the glistering ferns gave them a wispy look and they seemed to quiver with the drumbeats that were still beating in his ears.

He looked up and saw a young lady appearing from the distance with a basket on her head. He moved towards her and realised that she looked like his 'Mapuka' lady - her slenderness and grace as she walked. These native women seemed to have a magic that he could not resist. He smiled at her and she smiled back, a shy smile. He extended his hands to her and she took it. She was trying to take back her hand but he couldn't let go - he couldn't let go of this undeniably alluring woman.

Desire surged through him, heating his blood. His mouth descended on hers in a fierce kiss. She squirmed against him, trying to break his hold and drag her mouth from the intruding possession of his tongue and lips. Her struggle excited him. His arms tightened around her waist and she dropped her basket, her eyes wide with fear.

"Mame ko!" She was shouting and he knew she was asking him to let her go but he could not. Like a possessed man, he dragged her to the edge of the bushes and pinned her to the ground. She struggled like a rabbit captured in a trap as his body shamelessly stole the pleasures of hers with flaming expertise.

He eventually let her go and she scurried off crying. He did not regret the short but sweet moment of satiation. He now felt some release from the dark feelings that had possessed him. He knew he would never forget his native adventure. He stretched gratifyingly, suddenly feeling sleepy and began to make his way to Tenkora's guest-house. A sharp hiss drew his attention and he turned his back to see a large black shiny python wading in the water towards him.

The snake crossed the pond and came up to the bank. Its eyes were shining like bright, black beads, and its forked tongue was playing before it like a small flame. In the silence of the night, its hiss could be heard some distance inland, and in that sharp hiss, there was a warning, a threat.

....

The whole village seemed to be in mourning after the news of Domo's rape was heard. Timo was in great remorse. How could these men from the Trade Centre have turned out to be such traitors after they had given them large portions of their land to farm and to build this cocoa processing factory. Everyone suspected that it was the white investor from the Trade Centre who had done this hideous act. True, there were other white people living in the outskirts of the village but they were missionaries, working for respectable foreign non-governmental organisation. They were people who were doing good work within the village. They hardly ever troubled the villagers except whenever they wanted to offer some good advice. From Domo's description, it could only have been Tenkora's white man.

Tears streamed down the face of Mara, Domo's fiancé. "Papa, how could you have allowed these people to come to our land and rape my bride to be."

"I didn't know they were bad people. I thought they were here to help us. They brought those machines and they started plans for that factory. I wanted our land to prosper."

"Kai! Those people are not going to build any factory on our land – not today or tomorrow. They have defiled the soil." Mara stated vehemently.

The others agreed with him. "We cannot allow them to gain any stronghold on our land. Let them take their plans somewhere else."

"What do we do with their machines? We haven't finished paying for them."

"Let them take their machines away. We were doing allright without them. They are traitors!"

"But the man has built a house at the outskirts of our village. Do we continue to allow him to live there?"

"We'll have to get rid of them. They have raped a daughter of this village and broken a sacred oath by performing a sex act in the territory of the river god."

"First, we must perform certain rituals to purify this village or be cursed. Domo must be sent to the shrine of the river god with ten goats for pacification."

"Has Tenkora donated the ten goats and sheep as requested?" Timo asked.

"He was courageous enough to refuse to do this when requested at the chief's palace" Sessou interjected furiously. "I told you those men were up to no good!"

"What can we do now?" Mara asked angrily.

"We will drive them out of this land!" Sessou declared, raising his fists.

The angry men came flew at Tenkora, Tortison and Rizo with sticks and matchets as they hurriedly boarded their land rover. They were bellowing in a language Tortison didn't need to understand in order to understand what they were angry at. The strong flames of anger that were lashed out at them from their harsh voices, made Tortison's drive unsteadily as he zigzagged on the road, trying to escape from the town. As the mob broke up into two to surround their vehicle, Tortison saw his chance – He sped away at high speed, never to return to the town again.

....

Mr. Tiko reels in shock when the news of the rape incident at Afiram plains, his cherished homeland, reached him.

"I made Tenkora Babanda what he is and he is now trying to ruin me! How could he take these investors to go and abuse my beloved land?"

Sigoru, who brought the news shakes his head in reply.

"I want to see Tenkora Babanda suffer! An eye for an eye. He has repaid all my kindness with contempt."

"But he is married to your daughter." Sigoru states gravely.

"And he has brought only misery to her life!"

Dangerous emotions tear him apart and the adrenaline rushes too fast through his body and causes a tight pain in his chest.

"Then you would say that he was an opportunist?"

"He is worse than that. He is a hypocrite, a thief, a bastard, a _"

Mr. Tiko's voice breaks as he feels a searing pain shoot up his chest to his shoulder.

He loses his balance and tumbles backward to the ground. He panics, trying to reach for the table for support but the air is knocked out of his lungs and he lets out a sharp groan and goes limp.

CHAPTER 6

The Muno hospital was a small private hospital, concrete square built with gleaming glass and polished wood. It was a modern building, although it appeared rather bleak.

Serena had been informed that her father had had a stroke and had been rushed to the hospital. She was anxious to see his condition. It was a shock when the doctor announced that her father's condition was fatal.

"I am so sorry...his heart is very weak......."

"Please don't let daddy die."

"I am sorry, he may be leaving us soon."

Serena rushed to the hospital bed where her father lay dying. The room was heavy with grief. The minute he saw Serena, he asked all other visitors to go away and they reluctantly left. When they had gone out, he waved Serena to a chair. He spoke with difficulty.

Serena opened her mouth to speak but he waved his hands to stop her.

"I know you have had a very unhappy marriage and I know I am responsible for this. I put so much pressure on you to marry this man who I thought would make you happy but I can see the pain in your eyes. Can you forgive me?"

"Daddy, I forgive you. I don't blame you for my misfortune. You didn't know Tenkora would turn out to be the way he is."

"Have a child, Serena. Find another man and have a child."

"Father, I have almost lost hope."

"Serena, you must try to find happiness."

"Father, please don't die."

"You are asking a hard thing, Serena. I don't want to die but my breath is short and my hours are numbered. However, I could die peacefully if I knew that you would be happy."

"Oh daddy, I would be happy if you would live."

"I know Adendo Bilay once wanted to marry you and I stopped him. I heard that he is now divorced. Do you still love him Serena?"

"Yes. But I......"

"Then marry ……..him….. Serena. Divorce Tenkora and marry...." He suddenly stopped in the middle of his speech as if choking on something that lay deep within his throat. He coughed violently.

There was a moment of tense silence as Tenkora walked into the hospital room.

"Papa." Tenkora whispered as he knelt beside him.

"You have no shame Tenkora. I made you who you are and this is how you repay me. All I wanted from you in return was for you to make my daughter happy, to continue my lineage… you failed in both. Now you turn round to insult me!"

"No Papa, I have been grateful –"

"Get out of this place now Tenkora and don't come to my funeral when I die. Leave now, you cursed man!"

Tenkora reeled at the strong words and stormed out of the room indignantly.

The door was suddenly opened and the Reverend Minister, Serena's stepmother and Aunt Tami entered the room. The Reverend Minister walked to the bedside.

Mr. Tiko's breath heaved. It rattled in his throat. With great effort, he caught hold of life and held it back till he could speak.

'Please Reverend Minister, before I go, I would like you to grant me one last request. Take care of my Serena for me. See to it that she marries a man who loves her and who would give her children along with happiness."

With this he raised himself in the bed and sat shivering with the arms of death around him. The Reverend Minister began to pray, making the sign of the cross over him.

"I love you all." he pronounced casting one last look at all his loved ones gathered around him. His shoulder suddenly slumped as he fell back on his pillow, dying with a faint smile lingering on his lips.

There was a simultaneous outbreak of loud, forlorn wailing and inarticulate sobs and cries were alternated as expressions of grief. Serena quietly slipped out of the room as the lamentations grew louder.

....

At the Holy Spirit Church, the mass was nearly over. The soloist was singing: "Here am I Lord." and the casket was being lifted down the aisle. It was a huge and expensive funeral, very well attended by politicians, journalists and representatives of various groups who had had association with Mr. Tiko during his lifetime. Friends and acquaintances had also come from all over to accompany her father to his final resting-place.

Her father's grave was dug in the cemetery in which the members of her clan were buried, beside that of her mother's. Serena forced herself not to cry as the final prayers were read but she could not withhold the tears that poured and mingled with the heavy torrents of rain that began to fall from the sky.

"Give me hope." She cried out to God.

"You deserve so much happiness." Her father's words came to her.

The funeral reception was soon over and only those closest to the family remained at the family home. Serena, her two step-sisters, step-mother, Aunt Tami and three other relatives sat silently in the sitting room, their eyes filled with emotional messages of grief for the loss of Mr. Tiko.

The silence was broken by a knock on the door. Serena was pleasantly surprised to see Adendo as she opened the door.

"Have my condolences." Adendo said quietly.

They all nodded and Serena excused herself to talk to Adendo outside.

"It's all over the place that Tenkora is responsible for the death of my father." Serena confided in Adendo, her heart thundering with pain.

Serena's aching heart cried desperately to be filled only with the most gentle and joyous of love. She needed to conquer the bitterness and rage she was feeling towards Tenkora for being responsible for the sudden death of her father."

"I feel so sad, Adendo. I feel sad for the loss of my father and sad because I am still married to Tenkora and have to go back home to him."

"Don't be sad. Maybe you can forgive Tenkora after you talk to him. I'm sure he didn't realize that things would turn this way."

"He was always eager to get his hands on that land. He hurried my father to his death."

"I noticed he wasn't at the funeral. Maybe he would be remorseful enough to forget the land and start thinking about you."

"But my heart is aching so much Adendo."

"I'll be happy to sit here and mourn with you all night if you like."

Serena suddenly felt her angry emotions begin to miraculously melt away at the gentleness of Adendo's soft voice. "Thank you. I would like to talk a little longer."

Adendo was touching a part of her that had survived the ravages of the past, a delicate and hopeful place in her heart that had miraculously escaped unscarred. He wanted to seal those hurts and protect her from future pain. He lovingly convinced her that her life could be filled with happiness even after she had given up hope.

They talked, sharing quiet, important words and emotions, until finally, reluctantly, Adendo realized that he had to leave Serena to get some sleep.

"I'll come and visit you tomorrow." Adendo promised.

"I will be going back home." Serena said, her heart a tight ball of pain that she could not meet Adendo that often after she was back in Tenkora's house.

"We still have to talk some more. I will call you. Maybe we can meet again."

Serena nodded happily. She lifted her beautiful face and whispered: "Thank you."

....

Agony still burnt in Serena's heart as she returned left the family home for her own home. It was like a wild clanging of a bell. She moaned, feeling a sensation of utter chaos. entering the front door of their home as if dazed.

Her eye caught sight of a woman's handbag lying on the sofa. She picked it up surprised. There was a woman in the house!

Her heart pounding against her chest, she sniffed the trail of perfume towards the stairway, hoping that this was just from her imagination. More fevered now by her anticipation, she climbed up the stairs and paused behind the bedroom door where the perfume led her. She locked her fingers and strained her trembling hands on her head with a hysterical sob as she heard noises coming from the bedroom. "Oh God, please don't let this be my worst nightmare coming true.' She prayed.

Serena did not know the courage that had led her to open the door and the actions that carried her through on this memorable afternoon of her life. Her head sank upon her bosom as she beheld Tenkora and Alima making love on their marital bed. The breath, which had been bated in suspense was now exhaled in the form of a whispering wail: 'oh-h-h'. The suddenly silent room added to the length of the moment as the pair of naked bodies quickly disengaged to stare at her in surprise. At the end of a short though undefined time, she found herself slamming the door and running down the stairs, quivering with emotion. Tears blinded her eyes and an excruciating pulsation in her brain.

It was best to know the worst and she knew it now!'

All her strong feelings now seemed gathered together. Feelings of revulsion and indignance flooded over her as she thought about all she had sacrificed in her loveless marriage.

I will divorce Tenkora. The unexpected resolution came to her.

....

A loud thudding noise jolted Adendo out of his absorption in the morning's newspaper. He got up and walked to the reception area, where the noise came from. He found Juy Ross, a well-respected businessman and affiliate of the Trade Centre thumping the receptionist's table angrily as he shouted:

"You officials at the Trade Centre are totally corrupt!"

Adendo walked over to him, putting his arms around him to lead him to the interview room, which was more secluded.

"Calm down, Juy and let me know your problem."

"You make excessive insistence on formalities of all sorts to frustrate us businessmen. Then we are forced to give bribes in order to collect our documents."

"You must be wrong Juy. I would have known about this." Adendo stated, surprised at Mr. Ross's utterances.

"Are you sleeping?" Juy begun waving his arms.

Adendo finally managed to get him into the interview room, which was at the far end of the corridor and sat him down.

"I sent cocoa beans worth seventy thousand dollars through the Trade Centre to be sold to the American Trade partners. I have received a fax telling me that about sixty percent of my consignment is unwholesome. There is no way I can check the validity of this claim."

"What?"

"To finish me off, they are also claiming that because of the influx of cocoa beans on the market the price that we had negotiate had slumped by 30 percent and that they were not sure that all that was sent would be used immediately so I should expect less. I tell you, you people have knocked me out of the export game."

Adendo was shocked at this revelation.

"I know you are trying to cut off after you decided to give those investors from Nigeria the first refusal of the cocoa beans."

"You mean -"

"Yes, I mean, you people are trying to cripple my business, even when my price was good."

The realisation dawned on Adendo that Tenkora had been throwing dust in his eyes. He swore angrily." Look here, I knew nothing about this."

" Where do you find an incorruptible man in Ghana?"

"I am here." Adendo proffered, offering his hand.

"Then they are going to throw you out. You don't fit in there."

Adendo was speechless. Juy's Ross's concluding words were a slap in the face:

"You are a manager of an organization that is clumsy, rigid, sluggish, uncompetitive, uncreative, inefficient, disdainful of customer's needs and losing money!"

Adendo clutched his fists angrily. Tortison and Rizo were the ones playing it dirty. And this must be because they had come in the easy and unwholesome way. Tenkora had to provide some answers!

Adendo walked into Tenkora's office, not bothering to knock.

"Enough of these shady deals with foreigners that are depleting the resources of our land."

Tenkora looked him squarely in the face, unperturbed. " Are you condemning my efforts to establish external contacts for the Trade Centre of which you are a beneficiary?"

"I am not against external contacts. But what do we do with all this corruption? Who sanctioned those deals with Tortison and Rizo anyway?"

"I did." Tenkora lowered his eyes and began to tap the table with his pen, nervously.

"You said nothing about this part of the contract. I have had to find out myself - the hard way!"

"I would have told you….." Tenkora scratched his head guiltily.

"Cocoa beans are being exported at a faster rate than before but we do not see any improvements in the coffers. Where is all the money going, Tenkora?" Adendo demanded angrily.

"Where do you think your salary raise came from?"

"Dirty money?" Adendo asked appalled.

"I as Chief Executive Officer of the Trade Centre may not be perfect but the fact that you draw a payroll check from the Trade Centre means you don't have the freedom to …."

"To what? Tell you the obvious truth?"

"Keep the truth to yourself, Adendo. I know what I am doing."

You have…. You…" Adendo groped for a word, comment, anything to convince Tenkora that he was treading on dangerous grounds. It eluded him. Looking at Tenkora thoughtfully, he silently walked out of the room.

CHAPTER 7

In the lobby of one of the finest hotels in Ghana, the conference soliciting investors for the 'Cocoa Processing fund' was being held. The Hotel was situated at a beach resort and was vaulted, paneled and decorated with superb ornamentation lavishly displaying the rich culture of Ghana.

Some of the elaborate dressed men and women who descended from their Mercedes Benz cars did not only have the aura of snobbery, but the titles they carried before their names spoke of great wealth and power. Guests had been selected from a database collection of people that appeared to be the best prospects for the fund. It was by no means a comprehensive list of most of the wealthy people in Ghana. It however represented highly rich and sophisticated people - individuals and institutions who could throw cash around.

The theme of the conference aptly chosen was: **"Come, let's grow Ghana."**

Tenkora appeared very convincing in his blue suit, white silk shirt and red polka-dotted tie and a fully fringed handkerchief hang out like a flower from his breast pocket. He spoke with conviction.

"You will receive three times your money after a year. Imagine that! What bank would ever give you such returns?"

There was a sudden silence as people swallowed the wonderful offer like rich, refreshing wine. The silence was quickly broken with excited mutterings. Tenkora raised his hands to silence the crowd, the knowing smile on his face telling them that there was more good news to come.

"Many of you are asking yourselves: How are they going to achieve this outstanding success? Funds would be invested in rapidly growing areas, not only locally, but also abroad with quick and substantial gains made. You will then have your money back with the delicious cream topping whilst we use what is left to grow the economy....."

A hands shot up:

"But how do you intend to develop an economy that has been on the decline for many years and is right now is in a state of crisis?"

"We will do it this way. We will use the proceeds of our investments to support a program for the construction and operation of a cocoa-processing factory. We would also make available post harvest and cold store facilities for other national food crops." Tenkora answered confidently.

The soon-to-be-investors listened with interest. They were impressed with this excellent financial offer - one needed to maximize one's wealth by investing a fund like this........

The talk was soon over after people had been given the details on how to invest their money in the 'National Growth' fund in exchange for some certificates which they were to present on the day of maturity.

There were huge grins as people mentally made their financial calculations.

Later, analysts would puzzle over two enigmas. The first was how a grossly inadequate, under performing machinery at the Trade Centre could manage such a sophisticated fund. The second was how sophisticated people could have expected such huge returns on their investments in such a short time.

....

Tortison and Rizo grinned triumphantly when they looked at the bank statement featuring the large amounts people had invested in the 'investment fund'.

"We now have to look for land on which to build the cocoa processing factory". Tenkora said. Tortison exchanged a look with Rizo, which Tenkora did not understand.

"Rizo can I have a word?" Tenkora asked and walked out of the room with Rizo.

Just then, Alima walked in to serve some coffee. As Tortison admired her protruding backside he remembered the Mapuka dance, which had sent electric shocks through his spine and mesmerised him.

It was a shock to Alima when Tortison took her by the shoulders and kissed her. She however responded with unexpected enthusiasm. He grabbed her by her long artificial stresses and pulling her head downwards and took her mouth in an endless kiss that took her breath. His grip in her hair loosened as his long finger slid downward, showering caresses all over her body.

"Hmmm!" She whispered delighted

They found themselves yielding to the sensual pleasure. It was a jolt of wild sensation and a fever of dazed yearning as they kissed each other in a wild, exciting and forbidding rhythm.

Tortison cursed as they heard Tenkora and Rizo walking towards the room. He released his hold on Alima and they exchanged looks, knowing that there were still more fantasies yet to be explored.

"Tenkora is not happy with your time frame of three years. He would like to see the factory built before the elections in December this year." Rizo announced to Tortison.

"You have your facts mixed up here." Tortison replied. "We are supposed to invest the investors' money to yield some profit for them before we embark on the project."

"Well, you said the leasing company paid interest every six months. Invest it for only six months. We will pay out interest to the investors. Then we will build the factory in another four months then hopefully start the processing of cocoa from which we can earn revenue to pay out more interest.

Tortison was pensive for a while then replied: "All right. We will see what we can do."

"I would like most of the materials for the factory to be imported from abroad."

"This is just what we have in the estimates." Rizo stated, opening up the business plan for Tenkora to examine.

Tenkora smiled as he looked at it. He knew he was definitely on the road to fame.

"We'll take out our usual ten percent of course." He stated, smiling at his partners.

....

Serena wept as she packed all her prized possessions – jewellery, clothes, make-up, perfume, books and art collections into one single suitcase. She felt the need to leave the house immediately. She was resolved not to spend another day in the house. After packing her things, she indulged herself in bouts of weeping and after a while she wiped her tears indignantly. Tears were a luxury she couldn't afford at the moment. They were no good to her. They couldn't change the past, they couldn't heal the present and they couldn't alter the future. Blinking away the few that had formed again, she picked up her suitcase and walked resolutely out of the room.

It was about seven thirty in the evening when Serena arrived at Adendo's house. She came here because she didn't know where else to go, who else to trust.

"Serena!" Adendo exclaimed in surprise when he saw her holding the suitcase. "Where are you going?"

"I have left home. " She stated blandly. "I caught Tenkora in bed with his secretary."

Adendo opened his mouth shocked.

"I just want somewhere to spend the night until tomorrow when I would leave for my for the Afiram plains where my father left me property."

"Of course you can stay here." Adendo said, taking her suitcase from her and leading her inside the house."

"I will rather stay here in the garden for a while if you don't mind." She said. "I would like some fresh air."

Serena relaxed happily under the breezy pine tree when Adendo consented. Adendo took the suitcase inside and returned with a glass of fresh lemonade. She drank it slowly while Adendo watched her. Suddenly, he removed the glass from her hand and drew her into a big hug.

"I told you I would always take care of you, didn't I Serena?" He said huskily.

Serena snuggled closer, grateful for some comfort. Then quite suddenly, she felt it: the immense power of the emotions that Adendo had kept so carefully hidden, buried deep inside. It was almost as if her frustration, helplessness and torment were being felt by him too.

"After a moment she said bravely. "I have realised that I need to divorce Tenkora and I am going to do it."

"Oh I am so happy." Adendo confessed, as he turned his eyes to meet her solemn and beautiful eyes. Then more softly, he made another confession. "I have been longing for this to happen, especially when I realised that he didn't love you."

Now, as his dark, sensuous eyes gazed into hers, the fluttering of their hearts fanned the powerful emotions out of hiding, and the longing came to surface, defiant and unbridled. In that moment, Serena saw Adendo's desire for her, an intense desire that had began many years back and reached far beyond that moment. He cupped her head and not able to resist himself placed his mouth on hers and began to kiss her passionately. Serena mastered the will to pull away, averting her face. They both seemed out of breath with the passion that was being aroused between them.

Rebellion welled up in Adendo. "Don't feel guilty about what is between us. You know Tenkora does not love you and you are about to get a divorce."

Serena shook her head remorsefully. "But I am not yet divorced."

Adendo struggled to understand her remorse but he could not understand her, nor stop wanting her.

"Serena, I kissed you, nothing more. What is wrong with that? We have not committed adultery like he has done."

Serena was crying silently with her sweet-smelling hair against his chest.

"You don't want us to get romantic until the divorce is over? Is that it?" He asked quietly.

She nodded. "Yes, and also…"

"And also what?" You don't feel the same way for me?"

"It's not you, Adendo. It's me. Please believe me. I just need time to sort out my feelings."

Adendo withdrew as if his hands had been burnt, frustration welling up in his eyes. He still couldn't understand her. He wanted her to lean on him but she still seemed afraid to do so.

"I will always be there for you Serena. You must always remember that." He said, making gentle caressing movements behind her back as he again drew her to his chest.

Serena welcomed the warmth of his caresses and again snuggled closer.

The deep, startling voice of Tenkora behind them suddenly tore them apart.

"I was right. I knew I would find you here! In the arms of your lover, my bosom friend." Tenkora shouted out with indignation as he witnessed their embrace. They joined their hands and faced Tenkora like mourners around a grave. Tenkora's indignation gave way to fury as he walked toward the large pine tree where they stood. He threw out his hands, aiming straight at Serena, feeling rage build with his blow. In his entire married life he had never felt the urge to beat Serena as he wanted to do now. It was a compelling need to disfigure her deceitful face for daring to be unfaithful to him. He wanted to see her crumple and whimper. But Serena stood strong as she blocked the blow with her hand.

"Don't you dare touch her." Adendo moved to stand between them to defend her.

"You are not ashamed to defend her. Move away, you hypocrite! This is a woman that wants to destroy my life."

"I am quite certain that it is you that has destroyed hers."

"I gave her everything she needed and she gave me nothing! Not a child, not even the property that could advance my career."

"You gave me nothing that I wanted, Tenkora. Not love, no warmth and you ended up being unfaithful to me with your secretary. I have always been faithful to you."

"Liar! Then what are you doing her with Adendo?"

"He is my friend. He cares about me and he was just offering somewhere to stay until I return to the Afiram plains."

"Ah so that is what it is. You were competing with me for that property. The two of you set me up!"

"Nobody set you up Tenkora. You have been a long-time friend but Serena is also my friend and I would not have you maltreat her. I have not been unfaithful to you as a friend and neither has Serena. Would you not console a friend?"

Tenkora stared at them disbelievingly, grazed Serena disdainfully with his looks.

"You better come back home tonight or you are no longer my wife!" He shouted at her and stormed out of the house.

"I will go back home tonight." Serena explained gently Adendo after Tenkora had left. "I don't want it to go round that I have been unfaithful with you and I don't want to jeopardize your job at the Trade Centre."

Adendo's face fell when he realised that Serena was going to go back to Tenkora's house.

"Serena don't go back." He tried to convince her. "He would just hold on but continue to make you suffer."

But Serena was Adamant. Adendo fetched her suitcase.

"Don't drop me. I'll find my way." She insisted. Adendo watched her leave, his heart a tight ball of pain.

....

Serena changed her mind about going back to the home she had shared with Tenkora. She instead decided to go to Auntie Tami's, where she had left Ayisi for the past week.

She found Ayisi sleeping and she bent down to kiss him to rouse him up, caressing him fondly. Aunt Tami looked on impatiently as if bursting to tell her some important news before Ayisi woke up.

"What is it Aunt Tami?" Serena asked. "I hope Ayisi has not been an trouble. I will come for him immediately I settle down."

"You will not gain anything by leaving Tenkora at this stage, Serena." Aunt Tami admonished her. Just have a baby for him – I told you that it is only a mother who knows the father of her baby."

Serena shook her head vehemently. "No, Auntie. You know I can never do that. Moreover, I really want to be separated from

Tenkora. He doesn't make me happy. It is Adendo who makes me happy."

"So you want to leave him and marry Adendo?"

"I didn't say that." Serena crossed her hands in a sulking manner.

"My daughter, now is not the time to think about love, you must be thinking about future security, for yourself and for Ayisi and the unborn ones. Tenkora is a rich man – he has more prospects than Adendo."

"But I am not looking for money now, Auntie. I am so tired and I am just looking for love."

"How do you know that Adendo will love you the way you want? He may appear romantic but do you know why his wife left him? Has he told you the whole story?"

"I know he married a white woman and they did not get on well. But Auntie, you know he had wanted to marry me first and then –"

"And then you chose Tenkora. You married with your head, my daughter."

"Look, Auntie, let's stop talking about marriage. At the moment, I am so sick of it."

"Just remember one thing, my daughter. The devil you know is better than the angel you don't know!"

Serena was not sure what to make of this statement as she huddled Ayisi in hers arms.

"Mummy!" Ayisi shouted as he woke up and threw his arms around her neck.

"Oh my darling!" Serena said fondly, hugging him even tighter.

He was the only thing in the world that was truly hers now, the only person she could give love to and receive from freely with all her heart and she loved him as if he were her own!

....

Tenkora was perturbed when he received the divorce papers, sent to his office by Serena's lawyer.

So Serena wanted to divorce him because she was finding warmth in the arms of Adendo! The traitors!

The divorce papers said she was divorcing him on the grounds of infidelity. *If she was playing her role as a wife well, Alima might not have found her way into my bed!*

And the good news was that Alima had told him just yesterday that she was pregnant! E had been so overjoyed with the message that he had vowed to give her anything she wanted. He didn't care that she was demanding a new car and an apartment an he was ready to grant her strongest wish of marrying her. But curiously enough, he still didn't really want to lose Serena. She had been devoted all these years, docile and convenient. He was comfortable with her and her good looks and social graces made him fell good in public. And he didn't want to lose Afiram plains! He was planning to regain the hearts of the people. He had always yearned to possess that land. He scratched at his beard in confusion.

The messenger, who brought in the newspapers, interrupted Tenkora's brooding. Tenkora picked the newspapers and read and re-read the newspaper headlines in horror:

"Corruption at the Ghanaian Trade Centre."

A wave of nausea swept over him. He dared to read further what was being reported:

"Officials at the Ghanaian Trade Centre are cheating poor farmers and traders......."

Tenkora could not read any more. He threw the newspaper across the room and swore at the walls. A chill ran through his spine. For several minutes he sat motionless, dazed.

The telephone rang insistently. Tenkora imagined the worst. He picked up the phone reluctantly and discovered that it was the worst – it was the President!

"Hello, President Selabote here. What am I hearing, Babanda?" The President's voice boomed loudly over the phone.

"What is the problem, President?" Tenkora asked timidly.

"What do I hear about corruption at the Trade Centre?"

"C..corruption?" Tenkora stammered.

"Do you realise what this could mean? We could lose votes with the oncoming elections."

"It is a lie, Mr. President! Journalists who no longer do their jobs with the standards of integrity expected of them. It's all hype and sensationalism."

"What do you mean by a lie. I want the facts!" The President bellowed.

"It is an exaggeration of a minor case of deception we had to deal with from one of our officials and this has unfortunately been blown up."

"You must root out all corrupters now!,"

"I will do my best sir."

"I give you forty-eight hours." The President's final words resonated in Tenkora's ears as he placed down the receiver, shaking violently. His jaw fell slack.

Sweat broke out in droops on Tenkora's forehead. Who on earth could have reported the dealings going on at the Trade Centre, he wondered. Could it be Adendo who leaked out the information? He couldn't think of any enemy he had now apart from Adendo. He had been obsessed with this idea after he found him embracing his wife in his home. Adendo wanted to compete with him for all he had and was a threat. Therefore he had to leave!

Why not make Adendo the scapegoat? Adendo has succeeded with the farmers where you have failed. Adendo challenged you over the shady deals, Adendo has an eye for his wife….He fits the scapegoat scene perfectly!

Tenkora's hands suddenly shook at these cruel thoughts but he knew there was no going back. He had to get back to the President with a heroic story. He had to quickly arrange a meeting on Adendo's case.

....

Adendo sat facing the Board of the Trade Centre. People he had once considered his friends now appeared distant.

"I trusted you as a friend, Adendo," Tenkora spoke softly but with undertones of venom. " Now I know a malicious enemy is less to be feared than an avowed friend. You are now trying to ruin my reputation by spreading rumours about me."

Adendo stared at Tenkora, puzzled. "How have I spread rumours about you? You know I do not hide anything from you."

" Why do you Adendo, continuously side with the traders against the management of this organisation. Do you not realise how much you are undermining us - the whole Trade Board?" Mr. Egare asked patronizingly.

"I just want the work to succeed. I want things to be done the right way." Adendo spoke, his face set and voice firm.

"So if you are not on the side of the Board, whose side are you?" Mr. Egare quipped, tapping the side of his nose impatiently.

"Why put the question that way?" Adendo asked, mirroring his impatience. "If there is a problem, is it not stupid to breed opposition and enmity thereby multiplying our problems?"

"Who are you calling stupid?" Mr. Egare stood up angrily. "Someone is leaking information about the Trade Centre and there is no doubt that it is you."

"The President wants this traitor removed." Tenkora nodded in Mr. Egare's direction to assure him.

"I never sent any information to the Press and I'm certainly not a traitor." Adendo replied vehemently.

Tenkora shrugged. "You know Adendo, you have been dismissed from the Trade Centre, with effect from today on the grounds of gross disloyalty."

"What? ...." Adendo was suddenly aware of the futility of his own words and stopped talking. He got up and sickened by the expressions on the faces of those who were once his trusted colleagues, he silently walked out of the room.

Adendo's heart bled. Malice he realised was the one terrible trait which when openly portrayed sickened him. He had never imagined that the whole of the Trade Board could have been so corrupt.

He shook his head and turned his face to the skies, feeling as if his whole world had shattered at his feet.

CHAPTER 8

Adendo was shocked, hurt and devastated! He had worked so hard to advance the agricultural projects of the Trade Centre and he was being rewarded by such treachery from Tenkora. All he had wanted to do was make a significant contribution and he had never expected this to happen to him!

It was however at this very moment that Adendo decided to change his life. He was fed up with being a victim of life. He needed to turn things around – his career and his personal life. He was going to start his own business! He realised that what he loved to do and what he could do best was agricultural counseling and he was going to set up a company to do just that!

It was a painstaking move to start a company that would organize private farmers into a farmer's into a farmer's union and offer Agricultural extension services to them. After extensive marketing, he got ten private farmers to join the farmer's union, which he called the "Agripower". These private farmers did not depend on the Trade Centre for the development of their farms so Adendo had no concerns about crossing the path of Tenkora. He began his task by trying to meet the basic needs of the farmers.

He taught them how to build furrows around their farms to drain of excess water from heavy rains that would spoil their crops. He also taught them how to extract water from the soil to irrigate their farms when the rains were delayed or insufficient and he taught them how to insure their farms and farm produce to hedge against losses from bush fires.

Adendo's services was appreciated by the private large-scale farmers who began to perceive him as a focal point for concerns, ideas and networking. The result of all the hard work was highly organised plantations.

The more Adendo immersed himself, the more he found everything else falling into organized place. To Adendo, the private and independent farmer's union meant a valuable antidote to the corrupt influences of the Trade Centre. They were also the scene of labour and the strength of the farmers inspired him. It was a project in which he found a great deal of pleasure; an objective ambitious enough to make the time and energy worthwhile..

Soon, other private farmers across the country could not resist becoming a part of this exciting new wave of change in the agricultural sector of Ghana. Some farmers who depended solely on the Trade Centre drifted to join the 'Agripower'.

In the abundance of the harvest season, the lush fields became a picture of plenty. For the farmers belonging to 'Agripower' the earth had become a living thing, bountiful and rich.

....

It was like a divine intervention when Juy Ross called Adendo and asked him whether he was interested in a business proposition. Adendo couldn't wait to find out what business proposition Juy had to offer as he drove through the hilly regions to the *antelope plains*', where Juy's factory was situated.

He met Juy in the factory. He seemed nervous and strained.

Adendo looked round at the factory, impressed at what he saw.

Production was a four- step process. Fresh cut fruit carried to the receiving area of the packinghouse for trimming and pre-washing. Then conveyed through a segregating wall into hygienically air-conditioned packinghouse for peeling, coring and cutting. This was then placed on a conveyor belt passed through a hot water blancher and cooled under fresh water sprays. Fruits were then weighed into plastic containers, sealed and packed into shipping cases, which were stacked on pallets and loaded into a chiller, ready to be transported to the airport.

"Great business."

"Would you like to buy it? At least a large part of it." He clarified "I intend to maintain only fifteen percent shares."

Adendo wheeled round. He didn't believe that he had heard right.

"Why would you want to sell such a profitable business?"

"Profitable? I'm bankrupt. The Trade Centre saw to that."

"What? How bad is your financial situation?"

"The company is bleeding over seven hundred dollars at the bank. We have overdrawn our bank facility and the bank is demanding repayment."

"You don't have to give up so easily." Adendo tried to encourage him.

"I cannot cope with the frustrations in the business environment anymore." Juy suddenly appeared nervous and strained.

"I understand. Business in this economy is difficult. There are no easy answers, no certain direction. How much do you intend to sell the factory?"

"Well, I just told you that we owe the bank seven hundred thousand doltars."

"Seven hundred thousand dollars?" Adendo's voice came finally in a whispered gasp.

Adendo was pensive for some time and then replied. "That's a huge investment."

"Yes, it is."

"I don't know if I can meet your price. It is rather high."

"You must agree that this price is ridiculously low considering all I have invested in this business.

"I do agree. I would like to buy this factory." The decision suddenly came to Adendo.

"Well then, the offer is open for six hundred doltars if you agree to take it up before I leave for Meriga in two weeks" Juy Ross replied. "The paperwork on this will happen very quickly after you've paid the money."

Adendo faced a decision. He suddenly felt a new direction open in his life, a new point of interest. The question was what to do now? He thought about the possible risk but his mood of optimism prevailed. He decided to take up the challenge. He could have this excellent business offer at a ridiculously low price if he could take over it within two weeks. Two weeks?

Adendo got up early from his bed in deep thought.

It is a day of reckoning. I have to find a way of raising the funds to take up Juy Ross's offer.

He had a quick shower, dressed up and seated himself in his study with a notepad and pen in his hand.

He began by listing his assets. Having made a list of all the funds he had in the bank, along with investments, he added it up and found out that it came to three hundred thousand dollars. In all, he reckoned, he needed at least four thousand to make up the difference. There was only one thing he could do and he decided upon it without a moment's hesitation - borrow an amount of four hundred thousand dollars from the bank and use his house, which cost five hundred thousand dollars as collateral. The more the possibility of raising funds presented itself, the happier Adendo became.

....

"Serena, could you meet me for dinner at my favourite restaurant, the 'Journey Club house".

Adendo asked Serena over the phone, dying to tell her about the new opportunities that were open to them. He was excited when Serena agreed to meet him at the club house six-thirty.

The clubhouse had been built in a grand manner with a royal courtyard abounding with intricate carvings in stone, wood and terra-cotta surrounded by tropical greenery that added to the open-air a feel of a cool and spacious resting place. Amidst a multitude of red and purple bourgainville as were cascading waterfalls.

Serena suddenly felt very much at ease. She was not sure whether it was the environment that was intoxicating or Adendo himself. They were dining near the swimming pool in a lush garden, decorated with beautiful plants and surrounded by exquisite American art. Lovely music poured out from instruments played by a band and filled the garden. After a delicious dinner of assorted seafood, Serena relaxed completely with the lovely music in the background as she watched the fountain. She sat very still, absorbing the therapeutic music. Unobserved, Adendo watched the profile of her face from an angle. There was something ethereal about her as she sat there unmoving.

They stared quietly at each other. Now a quite different bond seemed to bind them together, two wounded people, each in need of some understanding and love.

Adendo whispered huskily: *"If you were my wife Serena, I would cherish you with my heart and soul. I would never look at another woman."*

Serena thought she saw a sheen of tears in his eyes, but she couldn't be certain because her own eyes were stinging with them.

Adendo suddenly took hold of her hands. "Serena, I have recently purchased a factory, a fruit processing factory."

"How wonderful!" She exclaimed, squeezing his hands tightly.

"It has come like a divine intervention. Think of the fact that we could now process the pineapples from your farm instead of trying to export them in their raw state, which has been so difficult."

Serena paused for a moment, feeling excited. "Are you asking me to be your business partner?" A feeling of being wanted by someone flooded over her – a sense of the binding and sustaining force of friendship in the midst of disappointment and loss.

Adendo had never seen Serena look so elated.

"She looks more beautiful than ever." He thought to himself. "Her sweet face and lips still have that same look of innocent truthfulness." He couldn't tear his eyes away from her. He wanted to prolong the moment, to etch this image of her on his mind and memory. *"She is like a dream, the dream I dreamed long ago and I am dreaming again."* As he gazed at her, a sharp longing for her shot through him. He felt again a powerful surge of tenderness.

"Yes, I am asking you to be my business partner and I would want much more. But I would leave that for later."

Serena was suddenly conscious of how attractive Adendo looked. She admired his look of rugged virility. She took a quick breath and caught the fragrance of his cologne, masculine and inviting. She was not only ready for this mental reunion; her heart was yearning for it. Judging from the appreciative glances that he was sending her way, she realized that he still found her attractive. *I feel like a flower blossoming under the sun of his attention. She smiled to herself.*

The romantic music filled with emotion and affection began to synchronize with Adendo's thoughts as he sipped his drink. The song being played rang out: "Love is what makes a man happy." It was a lilting song but the chords and words rang deep. The song seemed to communicate his desire for Serena:

"Wonderful sensations

When I look at you.

Powerful vibrations

When I hold you in my arms."

"Love is the sunlight of the soul." his eyes whispered to her along with the singers. She looked back at him.

"Do you remember all those wonderful days we spent together in Bendon?" He asked softly.

Serena nodded smiling, her eyes glowing.

"The memory has never left me...I loved you Serena. How I've often wondered the way things might have been between us...."

Serena instinctively reached out her hand to touch Adendo's face caressingly as she recalled the vivid images of the youthful days of friendship and pleasure.

"Would you like to dance?" Adendo asked Serena, as the power of the music became more compelling.

"I'd love to."

"You've always been a wonderful dancer." Adendo murmured, holding her close. Serena could not help reaching out her index finger to caress his cheek. "You're still remembering those days." She said softly.

"Yes, and I am also thinking of how happy you are making me now." He looked lovingly into her eyes. She felt his warm breath on her neck.

Serena felt a strange sensation in her heart. What a position for her to be placed in! She and Tenkora were not yet divorced and here she was, in the arms of another man and yet it felt all right. She began to feel light as a flood of emotion rushed through her. She couldn't deny the attraction inevitably drawing them together like a magnet. She thought to herself. *I feel good. I wish this could go on forever.*

By eleven o' clock p.m., as Serena lay in bed in her bed, she admitted to herself that it was the best night she had had in years. She could not help but relish it by going over everything in her mind. She recalled the way Adendo had looked at her, the turbulent emotions he had succeeded in arousing in her. She loved his looks and sense of humour. She loved the brisk authority in his deep voice and the confidence he exuded as he strode towards her. She loved the careless elegance with which he wore his clothes, the way his eyes gleamed when he was teasing her.

She wrapped her arms around her body, hugging herself. She pictured his face close to hers and tried to imagine what it would be like to lie next to him, in his arms, his body rubbing hers. She shivered, starting in surprise, annoyed at herself for harbouring such thoughts.

Should she take up the offer of being a partner in his company? Did she dare? Her heart was beating faster at the very prospect of doing anything so bold; she tried to picture herself in an office managing affairs, directing people.

I must be careful to show gratitude without encouragement, affection without commitment. I would rely on him for his individual support, but without leading him on, giving him the wrong impression. He must not misunderstand. He must not think I am looking for a husband. She cautioned herself.

Yet she clung to him, despite her foreboding, as the one patch of shade in the stormy moments of her life. She paused as she picked the telephone but only for a breath, her pulse beating as she dialed his number.

Adendo leaned back and thought of Serena and what she had said to him at the club, their dance... he listened to his heart pound against his chest as he remembered the scene.

Should he call her and tell her how much he enjoyed the evening? He debated.

He sat quietly for several moments by the telephone asking himself if he, Adendo Bilay knew what he was doing. To begin with, Serena was still battling with a divorce. Secondly, she was now a rich woman – the owner of large plantations and other properties. He didn't want any speculations about his intentions. He however could hardly go on denying now his pre-occupation with her. He picked up the phone suddenly and dialed her number.

After a long and enjoyable telephone conversation with Serena, Adendo lay in bed thinking what a pure delight it would be to have Serena by his side.

'Pure delight, pure delight, pure delight..." the phrase repeated itself in his mind until it struck a chord – A fruit dessert branded pure delight!'

Adendo became excited as he realized the trend of his inspiration.

Pineapple with mango and coconut topping a bit of vanilla or nutmeg........

He got up from his bed and sat for long hours at his desks drawing up a variety of fruit recipes. Bits of pineapples, pawpaw, guava, tangerines, mango, lemon, sweet apple and oranges blended with their juices and combined in various proportions to produce sweet-scented and attractive looking desserts.

'Passion delight', 'Tropical ecstasy', 'Mango miracle', 'Fruity paradise', 'Eden's guava', 'Pineapple extraordinaire', 'Fruity perfection', 'Tasty select', 'Relish Santana' and 'Fruity lips'

Adendo had never in his life felt so inspired.

CHAPTER 9

Eight o'clock, Monday morning, the new Chief Executive Officer of the 'Delico' company, Adendo Bilay, walked into the factory premises. The descending sun washed the open lawn with misty hues of yellow and orange. As always, the view had an inspiring effect on Adendo. No, purchasing this business hadn't been much of a gamble. Four hundred thousand dollars raised from the International Investment bank and all his investments and savings to make up the difference. Now he was a very broke but determined man.

The first few months of running the company was a great challenge for Adendo. He found the workers lacking some fundamental direction. Sales forecast was of very poor quality, production was slow, and processed fruit products from the factory did not justify their premium price and had not kept up with the competitive environment. Thus customer loyalty was low and on the decline.

There was hard work to be done to gain everyone's commitment and involvement.

It was one of the happiest day of Adendo's life when Serena walked into the factory premises to take up her seat as Managing Director of the company.

She looked startingly smart beautiful in a blue suit and white shirt and blue high-heeled shoes. Her hair was let down, falling gently in waves around her lovely face. Her light make-up accentuated her beauty.

"Wow! How would I be able to concentrate on my work with such a beautiful woman beside me." He said, half-teasing, half-serious.

She laughed merrily as he hugged her. Seeing apprehension in her eyes, Adendo guessed quietly. "You're nervous, aren't you?"

"Yes." She confessed. "It's so long since I worked in an office. I feel like a woman in a man's world."

"Now, it is Adendo and Serena's world and here there is only peace and love." Adendo replied softly.

His words were meant to put her at ease but they did not. Here she stood, with the man she had always loved, alone in the office. His romantic eyes studied her, appraising and obviously approving, she felt a rush of warmth but also, tremors of uncertainty.

Adendo felt unsettled too, struck anew by how beautiful and alluring she was. Here they were together, where they could learn more about each other and catch up on what they had missed in the past. But the uncertainty he saw in her eyes, made him realize that he had to move slowly.

Serena was his working colleague now. Which meant that for now, and for as long as she was, their relationship had to maintain some level of professionalism. She was also not yet divorced and he had his code of ethics and hers to maintain. He told her that with his eyes – that his attraction to her was still rife but that he trusted that time would bring them together to a point, where she would become his – at long last!

Serena understood the message and lowered her eyes.

"The contract we currently have is an order for five containers of sliced pineapples. Juy got us the contract from a supermarket in Meriga." Adendo changed the topic to business.

"Really?"

"Your role as a general manager is to co-ordinate the production and packaging, labelling, transporting, freight, quality control and custom formalities…..."

Adendo took Serena carefully through all the work rigmarole and explained her duties, responsibilities and authority carefully to her. He however made it clear that she was being given immense leeway to express her creativity and implement ideas that would lead to the success of the company.

Serena confronted her prospects with an emotional mix of determination and anxiety. She was amazed as she walked into the display room of the factory and saw what the workers could produce. It was like a delicatessen with a sweet smell of a variety of colourful fruit desserts.

Building rapport with the factory workers was easy. The workers liked Serena for her good nature, smart, bright appearance and bubbly personality that acted like a tonic on them, making them feel friendly and lighthearted. Soon, everyone started to speak in a free-and-easy tone that Serena had introduced.

....

It was a day to inspire confidence in anyone, with the invigorating breeze that carried the sweet smell of ripe mangoes from the trees that stood in the compound.

Serena looked round the plantation, which she had inherited from her father. The plantation looked loved, well tended and at peace. The savanna stretched some miles to the southward grew ever more crowded with vegetation.

Under Adendo's direction, they had managed to tame the land by replacing certain parts with chosen fruit. The curious growth of high matted and impenetrable grass was now growing citrus fruits. The open veldt with the dying trees was now growing pawpaw. The pineapple farm had been created with features that made the plantation distinctive among other farmlands: the land jutted out right to the water's edge on all sides so that the pineapples could always have water. All the farmers on the farm were now in profitable employment as out-growers for the factory.

Serena walked towards the truck, which was being loaded with fruit and smiled happily at Adendo who stood on the cart, receiving and arranging the cartons of pineapples, which were being thrown at him.

Serena climbed onto the truck to assist in counting the cartons. She seemed to work easily, cheerfully and with skill. The packing was swift and well organised. Adendo wished he could spare her the exertions. He heard her suddenly burst into a roar of laughter at something one of the farmers had said. Her face was all lit up.

Adendo wanted to share in Serena's laughter. As he looked into Serena's bubbling face, he suddenly realised that something was more important than the work he was doing - the happiness he experienced when Serena was around. Through Serena, he was having a greater insight into love: The will to love, the protectiveness of love, the grandeur of love.

After a hard day's work, they climbed the hills to the head of the farmlands, bordering the waterfalls, where stood a beautiful storey house. The long stretch of woodlands, fields and grassland had been cultivated into a large garden, rich in flowers and plants. There was a driveway dividing the front lawn, surrounded by thick green foliage.

"I understand Tenkora's passion for the Afiram plains." Adendo said quietly.

Serena stiffened at the mention of Tenkora. "I would like to rename this house." Serena said, changing the topic.

"The Serene gardens, of course, Adendo answered softly. This place reminds me of you – wonderfully tranquil and beautiful."

Serena smiled, pleased with the name. She led the way through the magnificent garden to the house.

"Make yourself at home." She declared as they entered the sitting room.

She could not have said anything that appealed to Adendo more. He reclined comfortably in the sofa, content just to wait for her as she went into her bedroom to take her shower.

Feeling relaxed after a bath, Serena dressed carefully in the new blue embroidered boubou and skirt she had purchased ealier that week, then decided a little make up was in order. She liked to look attractive around Adendo.

"Nice perfume." Adendo complimented her as she entered the room.

"Thank you. I will warm up some food."

Adendo watched Serena as she transported a delicious-looking meal from the kitchen on to the dining table. She was a woman who worked with care, her movements restful as she assembled table mats and napkins/ He breathed in the savoury aroma of the food that was placed in front of him. He was really hungry. Tentatively, he picked up his fork and knife and dug into the meal. Delicious! He thought as he chewed.

Serena caught the glimmer of admiration in Adendo's eyes. She smiled at him. The talked as they ate, words punctuates by long comfortable silences, about beautiful gardens and other inspiring topics.

Finally the words, or the silences, felt so comfortable that Adendo asked softly: "When will your divorce be completed."

Serena stiffened at the question. She suddenly seemed to begin an emotional journey as her lovely face filled up with sadness. She was silent for a while and Adendo could not bear her look of anguish. He walked towards her to put his arms around her.

"Is he refusing to sign the divorce papers?" He asked softly.

"The divorce could be completed after a year even if he doesn't sign but he has threatened to make it difficult for me." She replied.

"I can wait the year and I will stand by you whatever the difficulty." He said softly, looking gently into her eyes as he caressed her shoulders.

"I don't know Adendo. I have too many scars. They go too deep." Serena heaved a sigh.

"If you show me where the scars are, I will kiss them all away. I love you, Serena." He declared.

For a moment, they simply stared at each other, touching only with eyes that spoke so eloquently of their feelings for each other. Then she was in his arms and their lips found each other. In their kiss, there was something more than passion - there was gentle peace, joy and immense happiness.

....

Every day that Serena came to work, she seemed to share something very precious – something that was expressed with quiet words and gentle smiles. She felt so comfortable with Adendo and so wonderfully safe – a safety and comfort that went far beyond a friendship. Under his influence, her emotional scars were healing. For about a month, they seemed to bathe in each other's love and everything seemed so perfect until that horrible indictment appeared in the newspaper:

"BEST FRIEND STEALS MINISTER'S WIFE."

The story talked about how Adendo had betrayed Tenkora who had been his best friend, having an affair with his wife and luring her to divorce him. The words cut through Serena like the sharpest of knives, plunging like a knife into her already bleeding heart. She felt suddenly sad and bewildered. Tenkora was playing it dirty and cheapening the relationship between Adendo and herself. This news could also affect their business since it would reduce their credibility in the eyes of the public. She suddenly felt she had to get away from Adendo. There was no way their love could blossom under such malicious speculations.

She walked to Adendo's office with the newspapers and silently handed it to him. Adendo's heart churned angrily as he read the newspapers. A sudden frustration gave way to an emptiness, worse than his rage when Serena told him that she was resigning.

He saw anguish on her beautiful face and her lovely eyes glistened with tears.

"So you want to leave?"

"Yes." Serena admitted quietly, miserable, an acknowledgement that she may be making an irrational choice. Deep inside her, a voice was sending urgent warnings but her vulnerable situation terrified her and made her want to escape.

The message came with great pain, because Adendo knew now, that he could not subject Serena to such humiliation that would lower her reputation in the eyes of the public. He had to allow her to leave. He had to say good-bye to her and their magical love and friendship! He felt thrown back into the harsh and tormented world, denied of the quiet and gentle life of love with Serena.

"Adendo, I am sorry." She whispered.

"So am I Serena." Adendo replied as he walked out of the office to enter into a world of churning restlessness and monstrous emotions.

....

Aunt Tami looked at Serena with a raised eyebrow as if to tell her 'I told you so.'

"Auntie, I feel so devastated – How could Tenkora paint me like a cheap woman? How could he do this to me when it was he who was having the affair?"

"Serena, I told you to stay with your husband. You are rushing out of marriage into the arms of this man Adendo. What is he offering you apart from making you work for him."

"Auntie, Adendo did not make me work for him – he gave me a chance to know what I could be capable of. He believed in me."

"But now what is the result – he has lowered you in the eyes of society."

"Society, society, always society! It was I who cheapened myself by bowing to society and marrying Tenkora in the first place, when I did not love him. Auntie, don't you realize, the mistake was made ten year ago and I am now having to pay for it!" Her face contorted with pain, as she struggles with her memories. Her voice mirrored her anguish at the memory. It was a gasping memory of regret when she announced to Adendo that she was going to marry Tenkora. And there was more to the memory: the feeling of Adendo's arms around her, the warmth of his hugs and kisses, the wonderful feelings he aroused in her....

"Calm down my daughter. Look I will help you to build back your life – to stand strong as a woman!"

Aunt Tami kept her word when she sent Serena to one of the 23rd February women's meetings. It was a women's liberation movement formed by the Ex-first lady, Mrs. Zuzu. Each of the thirty women or so was dressed in extravagant clothing – laces and bright jewellery. These were women who were seeking to assume power in society. They chatted about world-changing topics and trivial ones, whilst sipping beer. To Serena, there seemed to be a void behind the arrogant airs.

"Women can definitely do better in positions of authority than men." The ex-first lady declared. "It is a competitive world and we must climb on the shoulders of the men to get what we want. What do you say Mrs. Babanda?"

All eyes turned on Serena as she was addressed. Most of the women seemed to have exchanged some gossip about her and were looking at her with a mixture of curiosity and apprehension.

"You all know Mrs. Babanda don't you?" The ex-lady introduced her. "Well, Mrs. Babanda – and she can still keep her married name if she wants – was bold enough to leave her rich husband for the man she loved."

"But that is still emotional dependency." One of the women interjected scornfully. "She must become successful in her own right!"

Serena cleared her throat. "There is more to the story than you know and I am looking to become independent."

The women made faces to demonstrate that they understood her plight – that of low self esteem. Serena prayed silently to be delivered from the cloud of self-pity that was rising up in her, knowing that if it overcame her, she would not be able to fight it.

"This woman's movement is your starting point." Mrs. Zuzu declared to her.

But Serena did not agree with her and she communicated this to Aunt Tami after the meeting: "I don't think I would like to be a member of this group."

"How can you say that Serena." Aunt Tami replied, shocked. "How do you think I was able to cope when my husband left me without any money or accommodation? It was this group which helped me to stand strong – to regain my dignity. You must take advantage of this opportunity."

But Serena at this moment did not feel like standing strong. Her heart only cried desperately for the love and friendship of Adendo.

....

The day was unusually warm for the time of the year – mid-June but Adendo was feeling cold as he jogged along the quiet path that lay in front of his house and inhaled the cool dawn air. The crisp air sent shivers of cold down his spine – or was it his thoughts?

Serena was always in his thoughts and now she was interwoven with his restless urgings, a phenomenon he had seemed to battle with ever since he met her. He needed her and that was plain and simple. He needed her because she had inspired him with a unique vision of love!

His thundering emotions subsided slightly with this thought and in the quiet, he began to hear the soft voices of his gentler emotions, trampled but still alive, urging him to go to her, to convince her to come back and work with him.

Serena had no wish to see Adendo. She felt strongly that their relationship could not know be a reality. Love was now a fragile and broken thing and she had to hold on to the shreds of her dignity – for her own sake and for Ayisi's. She knew the immense pain she would feel at seeing him would be too much to bear.

But Adendo's eyes looked uncertain and sad and compassion made Serena summon the courage to face him.

"Hello Adendo."

"Hello Serena."

"I wondered," he began softly. "I wondered if you could find the time for us to talk."

"About what, Adendo."

"About work."

"But I resigned."

"I know. But I have a business proposition and I need your help. I couldn't think of anyone else."

His voice was so gentle as he spoke.

Serena's damaged heart cried desperately to turn to Adendo and receive his gentle love but it seemed too difficult for her to conquer the fear and pain that so powerfully overwhelmed her. Their lovely dream of being together, even as business partners seemed so remote to her now. But then, quite suddenly, her heart was touched by a distant memory of love. Adendo's earnest eyes and soft voice brought back memories of the past when he had once proposed to her and she had rejected, much to her own detriment. Was she throwing away another chance? Her fears became more complicated but when she looked up to the man she loved, the answer came.

You can't go back! Her mind sent new and urgent warnings. I will go back! a defiant voice answered. I will go back!

'Allright Adendo. I will come back. What is the next move?"

"Oh, Serena, I am so grateful." Adendo whispered emotionally as his tender hands cupped her lovely face. His eyes met hers and mirrored her happiness. Yet there was something else that lay deep in Serena's eyes – pain and sadness.

"I love you Serena." He whispered in her ears. "And I am going to love you till all the sadness goes away."

Serena shifted slightly away. "What is this business proposition?"

"Serena, there is a prospect in Meriga interested in some of our products and I need to go and explore this market but I couldn't make this trip without you."

"A trip to Meriga? Why can't you go on your own?"

"Because I would be sure of success if you were by my side."

His pleading eyes were irresistible. Also, traveling to Meriga seemed like the change she badly needed. She couldn't find it in herself to refuse this offer. Instead she placed her hands in Adendo's and smiled up at him.

They exchanged another look of gentle warmth and their understanding went beyond words.

CHAPTER 10

Serena's heart quickened in delicious anticipation as the plane carried them off in swift silence to Meriga. The silence was soon broken by a recount from Adendo of the business they were going to negotiate in Meriga. Serena clung to every detail, grateful for this experience together with him. In a short while, there was a softening of his voice as he shifted the topic from business to personal as he quietly recounted their past days together in Bendon. Serena felt so greedy for the recounting of these memories – she wanted to laugh and talk and share. Adendo's smile, voice and touch were acting like a toxic on her.

Their long, luxurious conversation soon came to an end when after many hours, the plane landed in New Lark in Meriga. As the plane touched the tarmac, Serena felt a sudden and surprising eagerness for the experiences that lay ahead. They would explore the exciting and vibrant city together and they would close a business deal!

The Hotel in which they were staying the night was much larger than she had imagined and so beautifully decorated. Everything seemed so magical. Serena's eyes misted with emotion when she was greeted with a large bouquet of roses and a song of welcome from a pianist, who played skillfully on the piano.

"To show how much you are appreciated. Love, Adendo" The little card on the roses read and Serena was so touched to know that he had organized all this grand welcome for her.

She felt exhausted after unpacking and showering in her luxurious hotel room, but so very happy. For the first time, as she lay on her dreamy and lazy bed, she allowed herself the luxury to dream about love – the wonderful love that was unfolding once again between Adendo and herself.

It took Serena quite a while to select what to wear the next morning. Standing in front of the mirror, she looked stunning in a smart, esquisitely cut suit made of soft blue fabric, with a light blue floral print scarf tied around her neck. Her hair fell in soft waves around her face. She was satisfied with the effect – calm and sophisticated.

Adendo was dazzled by Serena's sophisticated appearance when he met her for breakfast. The cool beauty had given way to an even more beautiful one, elegant and alluring. He whistled under his breath and could not stop staring at her. He suddenly felt on top of the world, from the confidence he was feeling having her beside him. He felt that without a doubt, they were going to win this business deal.

It was with great anticipation that Serena and Adendo made their way to the office of their prospective client – Mr. Dillen, who owned 'The Sonaberries' a large chain of supermarkets in Meriga.

It was with a winning mixture of determination and hope, eloquence and brilliant salesmanship that Adendo made the presentation to Mr. Dillen and his management team about 'Delico' and the unique products they had to offer.

Adendo was like a small and excited schoolboy as he watched Mr. Dillen taste all fifteen varieties of their fruit desserts.

"'Passion delight', 'Tropical ecstasy', 'Mango miracle', 'Fruity paradise', 'Eden's guava', 'Pineapple extraordinaire', 'Fruity perfection', 'Tasty select', 'Relish Santana', 'Fruity lips', 'Pawpaw perfection', 'Fruit romance', 'Rainbow', "Sweet divine', 'Pine mine'. " he mentioned as he tasted them. The look on his face said it all.

"Yes, I love your products. These desserts are delightful! I want all fifteen varieties."

Mr. Dillen watched Adendo and Serena's faces light up. They exchanged a glance and a secret smile and he was amused. They were trying to hide their excitement. This may be their first major order and they might believe that if they showed too much enthusiasm, he might bargain for lower prices. He was definitely not going to do that. The products in his opinion were worth even much more than the prices they were quoting - three dollars for each fruit dessert.

They looked a little more than work partners - they seemed perfectly in tune. He wondered whether they had any plans of getting married but he didn't ask. He was preoccupied with signing the contract.

"It's seems like a wonderful dream Adendo." Serena exclaimed as they left Mr. Dillen's office. "I can't believe it's happening!"

"It's happening." Adendo said, giving her a hug. "And together, we will achieve much more."

....

After leaving Mr. Dillen's office, they decided to comb the city. Serena's athlete's body and shapely legs ate up the New Lark City effortlessly. They must have walked at least ten miles, combing the shops. After they had nearly worn themselves and the city out, Adendo decided to take Serena to the luxurious 'Greenfield' park, where he felt they could make the best of their limited time together abroad.

They feasted on a delicious array of sweet meats and rice ad drank a bottle of wine, laughing and aching pleasantly with the day's walking. Adendo was aware of feeling the most deeply about Serena when they were listening to jazz together after the meal. Unfeigned and open delight in each other flashed like heat lightning between them.

It was a time when Adendo felt was right to confide in Serena about the whole of his life. He felt that she was a stakeholder in his destiny – someone who could have previously been his wife and could still be his future wife. He told her in detail about his marriage and where it had failed. As he talked, she listened intently, so intently that he found himself telling the story of his life with great ease and great insight. She seemed to hang on every word!

"You deserve so much happiness in life Adendo" Serena empathised. "You are such a wonderful person. You have made such a difference in my life."

Adendo fed on the remark. Serena's gratitude made wonderful nourishment.

"If only I had married you Serena…If only you had accepted my proposal"

Serena fiddled with her hands nervously. "Please let's not discuss this topic anymore. I…I" She struggled with words.

"Y-you mentioned that you had a brother in New Lark. Does he live far away from here?" Serena asked, trying to change the topic.

"Well, not very far."

"Well, why haven't you thought of us visiting him?"

Adendo did not try to explain why he had no inclination to visit his brother, hoping Serena would assume that it was because there was insufficient time. But he could tell that she sensed the alienation between Jota and himself, though probably not knowing what had caused it, or how deeply it went.

Adendo's opposition to his brother was purely on moral grounds. Jota was disreputable; it was as simple as that. It was not so much the life he had led but the trouble it had caused him. He had spent many long years remitting money to Jota for a supposed operation, which had been a fabrication. Now he heard that Jota did recently have an operation. Although he was reluctant to reduce the pleasure of their trip by a visit to a controversial brother, he now felt it was his duty.

"All right, I guess we have to visit Jota since he lives just twenty minutes away from this park. But we won't be long."

They found Jota relaxing in a wheel chair in the comforts of his home. His apartment was modern but seemed a bit neglected. A large abstract painting dominated the decor of the room.

There could be no doubt that Jota and Adendo were brothers. They shared the same smooth features, dark eyes and fulsome lips. But there was a difference in composure that made Serena feel wary of Jota.

"Well, what a surprise to see you brother, after so many years of desertion." Jota greeted them with an indifference that surprised Serena.

"How are you Jota?" Adendo asked trying to embrace him. Jota did not answer but looked past Adendo at Serena. "And what do you have here? A new wife?"

"Meet Serena, my business partner." Adendo proffered.

Jota assessed her with appreciation, making ogling eyes at her to show that he thought she was more than a business partner to his brother. "She's beautiful. Is she available?"

Adendo looked away, sickened that his brother was not inspiring in him the congeniality he hoped a person just discharged from hospital would.

"Jota, I thought you had changed. I - "

He stopped short as a little boy ran into the room. Serena turned to Adendo. He looked as if he had seen a ghost!

A strange sound seemed to come from his throat, like a strangled voice as he clutched the boy's hands."

"He's not your son, he's not your son!" Jota was shouting, moving forward in his wheel chair to make an attempt to separate the two.

A lady run into the sitting room at the commotion.

"Adelina!" Adendo was now shouting like a mad man. "What are you doing with my brother?....You gave him this little boy?..."

"He does look very much like Terry, doesn't he?"

Upon seeing a boy that looked so much like his Terry, Adendo felt instant shock, then grief and rage. But of the necessary skills that Adendo had acquired during his many years of executive work, was the ability to hide his emotions when he had to.

"I didn't know that you left me for my brother." Adendo looked gravely at Adelina. "Why?" Adelina stared with a certain awe at her ex-husband.

Jota was looking up at the ceiling, touching and re-touching his fingertips together. For several moments, Adendo looked at him without speaking. Anger was growing inside him. It shifted rapidly from Adelina for having caused him so much misery and for marrying no other man than his brother and to have a child that looked so much like the one he had lost; to Jota for wanting what he had and for being so ungrateful and ruthless.

"Where are your standards, brother?" He asked Jota, disgusted.

"Why would I turn away your wife when she came to me? – She's family!" Jota drawled.

Adendo threw Jota one last sickening glance and then pulled Serena out through the door.

You're a wicked man." Serena could not keep herself from telling this man exactly what she thought of him before leaving.

Wicked. Jota reflected as he watched them leave. It was a word he had always been fond of from his early days.

....

As they sat in the plane back to Ghana, Serena searched Adendo's handsome face for proof that he was trying to avoid entering into any conversation of any sort with her. She was right – the dark eyes that met hers were cold and distant.

"You look so distant Adendo. Talk to me." She said soothingly.

"I'm angry and restless and consumed by ugly thoughts and emotions that overwhelm me – hatred and bitterness at the cruel trickery and deceit of my brother and ex-wife."

"I understand the way you feel…."

"I don't know if I can conquer these emotions even if I tried. I would only be grateful if you left me alone."

He could see the sad comprehension on he lovely face as he turned from her. Serena's fragile heart cried out for him, filled with pain. Perhaps she really had no permanent place in his world and he in hers, she decided. Their wonderful, breathtaking trip was now overshadowed with a dark cloud of sadness.

....

There had not been much interaction between Serena and Adendo during office hours for about a week after they had arrived from Meriga. Mr. Dillen had been honest with his word and had sent a deposit for a large order. With the renewable contract signed for with his company for a year, 'Delico' seemed to become a very big business in one gigantic leap. The success seemed so instantaneous and overwhelming. Suddenly, extra help had to be hired, more out-growers found.

What seemed so strange was the fact that Adendo still seemed too preoccupied to celebrate their success.

Could it be that he is thinking about Adelina. Could it be that he still loves her? Serena wondered.

Serena moved to Adendo as he sat in the conference room and placed her hands gently on his shoulder. As if pushed by inner restlessness, he left the conference table and walked to the window.

Truly, Adendo felt troubled. His felt suddenly wary about his growing love for Serena who had become so central to his life. His strong distrust for women had erupted strongly after seeing Adelina with his brother and this was the emotional conflict that was tearing him apart.

Serena decided to probe into Adendo's thoughts and walked towards him as he stood at the window. But there was an event happening outside that stole his immediate attention.

"What are these soldiers doing on our premises?" Adendo spoke suddenly. Serena rushed to the window to see what he was talking about. Flanked by several soldiers was a man they recognised as Mr. Sesu, the Deputy Minister for agriculture.

"Let's go and meet them." Adendo said. They walked out steadily to meet their uninvited guests.

"How may we help you sir?" Adendo asked Mr. Sesu.

"We have heard that your company is abusing the free zone facility by harbouring dubious foreign investors who are defrauding the local banks by false presentations.

"What on earth are you talking about?"

"We would like to examine what are in these trucks." Mr. Sesu demanded pointing to the truckloads ready for shipment.

Adendo ordered some workers to open the truck doors for inspection. The sweet scent of fruits assailed the air, drawing Mr. Sesu and his soldiers spontaneously to the carton boxes.

"What? fruit salads!" Mr. Sesu exclaimed as he picked up one container of fruit desserts. "My, these look so attractive. Do you produce these?"

"Of course!" Adendo answered. "Would you like to take a look round our factory?"

"You mean you produce all this here in Ghana?" Mr. Sesu asked. "But my friend, why haven't we seen this before?"

"Well you see they are mainly for export."

"And you have been keeping quiet about all this? But this is marvelous!"

After an hour at the factory, Mr. Sesu invited Adendo and Serena for dinner in his home the next evening. He obviously wanted to learn more about the business. Serena was apprehensive but Adendo felt great. His words were re-assuring.

"The 'Delico' company is on its way to great success and nobody can stop that!"

As the months went by, Serena and himself had a track record to point to; it was irrefutable.

People recommended them for being great entrepreneurs. They were flattered but reflected that their key success factor was their 'magic' order from Mr. Dillen. What was clear to them was that together they were spearheading an exciting change process within the factory. The level of morale within the factory couldn't have been higher. Personnel were finding elements in which they could function and were bringing out their best work under their leadership.

The only question that remained to be answered was whether Adendo and Serena could again love each other without inhibition, without the interference of a disturbing past.

....

Tenkora was too stunned at the events of the previous few days to be angry. Message was received that the leasing company in Meriga in which they had invested millions of dollars of public funds was folding up. They could no longer meet the huge interest payments. It was like discovering the world was coming to an end and there was nothing he could do about it.

This disaster could not have happened at a worse time. There was dire need of a large cash infusion or plans for the cocoa-processing factory would have to be shelved. Recriminations from the government and the public would soon be knocking at his door. Tenkora knew he had to play for time. The longer it took for official opinion to crystallize, the better.

He decided to read the 'Business in America' magazine to see whether he could obtain some news on interested investors, whom he could partner with to get out of this mess. He was stunned at what he saw when he opened the middle page.

What is this? A feature on Adendo!

A wave of nausea swept over him as he read the journalist's report.

"…..The 'Delico' company is making a great contribution to agriculture in this country through the export of attractively packaged fruit desserts, the first of its kind in the country. Such reformers are necessary because they complement the activities the government."

The story went on to talk about how Adendo was to receive an award for the best business agriculturist in Ghana. Tenkora felt a deep revulsion at the thought. He had never imagined that he could be so filled with revulsion at another man's success.

Tenkora swore as he threw the magazine into the waste paper basket. He had gone to great lengths to impress on the Minister of Agriculture that Adendo was funding his company with money from some illegal connections – they hadn't listened!

He gazed through the window of his office and exhaled slowly as he looked into the streets of Tendam. One of the most disagreeable features of Tenkora's position was that Adendo's name would soon be on everyone's lips. It would now become impossible to attend any important business conference without the risk of meeting him. This was how it was going to be, like a sore, which keeps knocking against something! What hurt him so much was the fact that Adendo was gulping down all his leftovers: using the land, which should have been rightfully his to make his money and making love to his wife!

CHAPTER 11

Arriving patrons of the Awards night filled the foyer of the Banquet hall. The subdued chatter of voices was punctuated by hearty greetings. The place was filled with dignitaries. Excitement grew as pleasantries were exchanged. People were savouring the light cocktail whilst walking around the foyer, chatting with friends and acquaintances they had not seen in a while.

Tenkora stared at Serena from across the crowded room, drawn by her arresting appearance. He could hardly recognise her as the Serena he knew. Wearing a dark blue and silver satin dress, adorned with pearls, which complemented her beautiful glowing skin and her shiny black hair falling around her face, Serena looked stunningly beautiful. Frowning at the change, he studied her closer. She was wearing her hair differently. Instead of it being tied back in a knot, it cascaded in a luxurious mass around her face and shoulders. The silver and blue evening gown she wore was strikingly chic and complemented the ripeness of her figure. He took a quick glance at Alima who was busy chatting to some friends and she paled into significance compared to Serena. This wasn't Serena. Tonight, she looked almost untouchable.

Serena's eyes caught that of Tenkora as they entered. He stood in the doorway, clasping a drink tightly in his hands as if he wanted to crash the glass. Her heart shrunk with withering contempt as he held her look. She realized that she no longer needed him or cared for him anymore and wondered how she could have agonized over a man whom she neither liked nor respected. She quickly turned her back to his gaze. But it was too late. Tenkora was walking towards her.

"I'm not going to ask if you have missed me. I can see you are being very well taken care of." he drawled.

"Missed you? I don't even see the need to talk to you. In just a month's time our divorce would be through and I would have no ties whatsoever with you." Serena replied casually.

"You could have taken a hint to come back when I refused to sign the divorce papers." Tenkora persevered. "And still, we could be friends."

"No, Tenkora. We were never friends before and we can't be now. Could you please excuse me." As Serena made a move to walk away, Tenkora quickly grabbed her by the arm. "What do you want from me, Serena? Am I supposed to crawl, beg or what before you hold a conversation with me?"

"I want absolutely nothing from you, Tenkora."

"Alima's pregnant." Tenkora went on. "She is having my baby – something you were never capable off. You deprived me of the very thing I wanted and now you are making love to my best friend!"

"Adendo is not your best friend and I am not sleeping with him. We are just business partners!" Serena hissed at Tenkora. But Tenkora wouldn't leave her alone. He grabbed her arm.

"Serena, you must appreciate what I was going through when I wanted my own son."

Adendo saw Tenkora hold Serenaas he walked towards them and for a second froze. Could it be that the two of them were getting re-united. Were they talking about getting together? He quickly dismissed the dark thoughts and walked up to where they stood in hurried strides.

"To what does my Executive Director owe this honour?" He asked Tenkora sarcastically.

Anger in him welled Tenkora as he sought to confront Adendo. "Do you believe in omens?" He asked.

Adendo composed his face into a frown of impatience. Tenkora, sensing his discomposure laughed a mirthless laugh.

"I have nothing to say to you." Adendo replied and pulled Serena away.

"But I have a few things to discuss with you." Tenkora put his arms on Adendo's shoulder to stop him. He took out an envelope from his suit, opened it and removed three pages, handing them to Adendo.

"What in God's name is this?"

"A proposal for a Partnership deal. Your company has performed admirably over the last year."

"Why in God's name would you even consider such a thing?" Adendo asked surprised.

"We think our business venture can benefit from your business links. We are also aware that your capital requirements are growing each day and you may need a little equity injection."

"Let me assure you, I don't have any problems with capital requirements." Adendo replied.

Adendo took the sheets carefully, folded it, and then proceeded to tear the fold in half. He held the torn paper out for Tenkora.

"Your first business is to return this to wherever it came from."

"We know you are fast becoming influential and powerful but we can give you the kind of wealth that would place you in the esteemed company of the most respectable entrepreneurs and dignitaries in the international world."

"Well, I do not seek to acquire wealth by robbing millions from the faceless public and leading the country to its financial death and still appear respectable in the process."

"I thought you had talent."

"I'm sorry, I do not have the killer instinct."

"Then you cannot be a bankable commodity in the international market."

"Am I not already making my own way?"

"Come on, take your chances in the ocean. Swim with the sharks." Tenkora coaxed.

" If I swim with the sharks, they may take a bite out of me. I choose to stay in my safe small pond."

"Adendo, you must see reason." Tenkora spoke out , looking disapprovingly at Adendo.

"I am sorry, I do not have the time. Please excuse me." Adendo turned to Serena and walked off with her into the banquet hall where people had started taking their seats.

They bumped into Mrs Zuzu as they walked up to their seats.

"Hello Mrs. Zuzu." Adendo greeted the ex- First lady. She ignored him and instead turned to Serena, eying her jewels.

"You have made the women's movement proud – you have been the brain behind two men who both want you and you know how to get rewarded. You know my dear – continue to play the two a little longer and you will soon be very rich."

Both Adendo and Serena froze at these words but there was no time for Serena to reply to them. The 'Delico company's name was being called out to receive their award.

Applause broke around them as Adendo was called to the stage to receive an award on behalf of the 'Delico' company. Tenkora watched Adendo and listened to his understated but confident words as he thanked 'the whole world' for his award and suddenly realized why he felt uncomfortable and anxious. Adendo was a man on his way up in the international business world. He carried himself with assurance. And now, there was one profound difference between he and Adendo and both of them knew it. Adendo was dealing from a position of strength represented by the trophy he held in his hands. He, Tenkora was not!

Adendo spent a sleepless night thinking about what Mrs. Zuzu had said to Serena. There were now questions about Serena – could it be that the lovely vulnerable woman whom he had grown to love so desperately never existed. Could the real Serena be a clever confident woman who was playing with him? He felt sad, confused, alone. Thoughts of Serena had danced in his mind until they were now ready to collapse. She had been in his thoughts almost every minute throughout each day, distracting him. But now he wanted to throw these tempting thoughts out and banish them forever. That gentle, tender place in his heart was gone now, trampled by monstrous emotions that raged within him now. He was resolute that he would allow Serena to leave – to go back to Tenkora.

He didn't trust himself not to succumb to his desperate need for her – a need that would only drown him further in the tormented depths of his disillusionment.

....

It was a breezy Saturday morning as Adendo drove with Serena towards the Afiram plains.

It was his intention to break the news to her that morning that their relationship had to end. He intended offering her some money to start a business of her own. He suddenly felt a deep emptiness. He wondered is Serena would have any regrets.

Des she regret that having married Tenkora and not me? Will she regret that our love has been belittled and made just a passing fancy? The questions were self-indulgent and self-destructive. His dark, handsome features settled into a somber grimness.

Serena sensed that there was something pressing on Adendo's mind. She tried to find peace in the tranquil scenery, but it was impossible, because she was so aware of him sitting by her side. Are his eyes smoldering with disdain of our relationship or with yearning for Adelina? Unable to see the shadowed messages of his stone-eyes was painful as the questions bombarded her, guided missiles that found their mark in her heart.

They drove in stifled silence, which masked off vulnerability and tucked fears away behind erected barriers. Adendo had been so absorbed in his thoughts that he did not notice the red jeep that was closely following their land rover and which was suddenly brought to a halt as it blocked their pathway.

Something wasn't right.

Two men descended from the vehicle. Adendo froze as Tenkora and Tortison descended from the vehicle.

Tortison walked up to Adendo and pointed his gun. "Get down." Adendo looked to see if Serena was all right - she looked as pale as a ghost. They both got down.

"Get into the car." Tortison demanded and shoved them into the back of the red jeep.

Anxious thoughts filled Adendo's mind. Where were they taking them?

For several hours they rode without anyone speaking. Adendo held on tightly to Serena's hands and stared straight ahead, fighting the urge to panic. After about three hours ride, they pulled up at the entrance of what looked like an isolated valley surrounded by thick foliage. They were pushed roughly outside the jeep.

Adendo held on tightly to Serena. As they walked deeper into the valley, Adendo saw that there was a waterfall gushing down from the huge rocks, which formed a dome around the valley, looming largely on top of them. The waterfalls were sure to drown any sound of guns being fired. Serena shivered.

"This is just an unplanned rendezvous to ask you to hand over to me what you have stolen from me." Tenkora said to Adendo,his eyes glistening with hostility.

"I have stolen nothing."

"I want back Serena and the Afiram plains." Tenkora snapped impatiently. "The two are mine!"

"No!" Serena shouted, bravely defiant. "It is only two weeks and our marriage will be automatically dissolved. That would be the end Tenkora. Accept it. I am never going to come back to you!'

"We'll see about that." He drawled. He beckoned to Tortison who pointed the gun at Serena and reached out to grab her.

"Leave her alone." Adendo ordered.

"There is a price." Tenkora's was becoming more heated.

"I'll pay."

Tenkora reached inside his jacket and brought out neatly folded sheets.

"This is a contract, skilfully prepared for you to hand over the Delico Company to us." He shoved the document at Adendo. "All you have to do is to sign."

"W-What?" Adendo stammered.

"We will not leave you destitute. You will receive some money for your efforts."

A chill went up Adendo's spine as Tenkora threw a golden-plaited pen at him. He did not catch it so it fell on the floor.

"No, Adendo No! Serena shouted. "How can you ask Adendo to hand over the factory, which he has toiled for to you? Are you crazy?"

"I'll show you how crazy I am. Get back into the car!" He ordered. Serena had never seen such a look of madness in Tenkora's eyes.

"No leave her alone. I will sign the contract." Adendo's action was immediate and decisive as he took the contract from Tenkora and proceeded to sign it. Serena's heart was aching, gasping, pleading as Adendo signed the contract. The thundering beat of her heart became suddenly still, just for a moment, but long enough for her to decide what to do. In a split of a second,

Serena bent down slowly as if to pick the pen and then in a flash of a second, the pen was hurled at Tortison's groin. An echo of rifle filled the air as Tortison howled in pain and clutched his groin. Serena kicked the gun out of his hand and it flew to lie some yards away. Tenkora rushed to in desperation to pick up the gun.

"Quick, let's run." Adendo said as he grabbed Serena to her feet.

Within the split of a second, they leapt like lightning, fleeing for their lives. A burst of gunfire filled the air. They ducked behind the waterfall into the belly of the rocks. More shots were being fired amidst angry shouts.

"Let's get to the top of the rocks." Adendo hissed.

They climbed up the rocks. The ground was very slippery yet all they could do now was run. After running for a while, they stopped and listened. They could hear no movement or talking behind them. An echo of rifle suddenly filled the air and they lay down motionless. They fought their way up. Adendo continuously pulled Serena up but soon his strength began to wane.

They climbed up the stony ridge and didn't stop until they were hundred yards away. Soon, they reached the top. The crack of fire from a gun rung in the air. There was nowhere else to go but to jump down to their death. Adendo felt doomed, finished. He sank to his knees and together they began to pray. After a long period of prayer, they realized that nothing had happened. They lay flat on the ground for what seemed like hours. Serena felt dirty and tired and pangs of hunger erupted in her stomach.

"Serena, you were so brave." Adendo hugged her with tenderness.

"It was your dream, Adendo, so generously shared with me. I couldn't let them take it away from you."

Their eyes met and held and there was an invisible power and their hearts fanned the powerful emotions out of hiding and all the love and longing came to the surface, brave and defiant.

Serena felt the immense power of the emotions that Adendo had kept so carefully hidden, buried deep inside.

After hours of waiting, they found a way to climb down to the bottom of the rocky crevice again. Still there was no movement anywhere. Carefully, they moved deeper into the trees. It was getting dark and they could hardly see their way through the forest.

Suddenly, they saw a light being shone searchingly around the area where they stood. The light changed position and headed right towards them. They recognised Tortison as he shone his light on them, his face lighting up as he saw them.

As he raised his gun to shoot at Adendo's leg, Tortison's eyes caught sight of a huge black shiny snake, such as the one he had seen in that river months ago. Images of his 'Mapuka' lady crept to him. He lowered his gun to shoot at it but before he could, the snake's sharp fangs sank deeply into his legs an delivered its deadly poison.

A look of pain crept into Tortison's face, turning quickly into repulsion. He grimaced and held his stomach, then turned and retched onto the rocks beside him. Wiping his mouth, he raised his gun again. He took several steps forward, then seemed to lose energy. The gun fell to the ground. He stumbled backward a few feet then collapsed to the ground.

"I think he's been bitten by a snake." Serena said, breathing heavily.

"Come, let's run." Adendo said, pulling Serena along.

They climbed over the rocks set in the ground, jumped down into the valley and ran through the tall grass. They did not break their pace until they came to a huge tree and upon reaching it, leaned against the tree, out of breath and panting with exertion.

Desperately tired, Serena and Adendo lay flat on the ground. Adendo held Serena tightly. The wind howled around them and stirred up the dirt and made them shiver with cold. After a while, Serena felt Adendo's hold on her slacken and realized he had fallen asleep.

Adendo slipped into a restless sleep during which he dreamed he and Serena were running desperately from an unknown enemy, certain that somewhere was a secret key that would open the way to safety. Then somewhere in the bushes, he saw the key. He reached out to retrieve it!

He jerked awake, sweating profusely.

It was almost dawn. Adendo remained awake. He could hardly sleep with Serena in his arms like this. His heart thumped against his chest. He wanted to tell her how much he loved her and how much he wanted her to be his wife. But was this the right time to make things more complicated? He reproached himself for his impatience and stupidity. He listened attentively to the noise of the jungle. Did he hear the hiss of a snake? He began to wonder if they would get out of the jungle alive.

"Adendo, Adendo, Adendo," Serena mumbled in her sleep and drew closer to him. She slid her hands into his shirt to ward off the cold and held him. Then suddenly, she began to cry silent tears that rolled down her face and wet Adendo's chest. He put his arms around her and held her close, murmuring tenderly into her ears to comfort her.

"I love you, Serena. You know that, don't you? Love conquers everything. I will protect you always."

She sniffed and clung tighter to him. Suddenly, overwhelmed by emotion, her need for him gave him the strength to say what he may never have had the chance to say under the circumstances: "Serena, would you marry me?"

Suddenly, as if he debarred from speaking those magic words, the heavens opened and rain began to pour from the sky. It thrashed though the trees and whipped their faces. Adendo jolted up and pulled Serena to her feet. Not able to withhold himself anymore, he whistled into the darkness. After a brief moment, they heard someone whistle in response. Their hearts leapt with joy. Cautiously, Adendo and Serena moved forward, Adendo whistling all the while.

From the corner of his eye, Adendo saw a movement in the trees towards his right. A man lurched suddenly in front of them.

"Who is it?" He asked in the local dialect.

"We are lost." Adendo replied. "Could you please lead us to the Afiram plains?"

"I am searching for those herbs to cure the heart disease of grandfather, which you all know must be picked before the dawn breaks……"

"We can wait." Serena replied, shivering with cold. The man looked on them sympathetically and suddenly said:

"Come with me. I will show you the way and then get the herbs."

They could hardly see his face in the dark. He was heavily muscled and except for a loincloth around his waist, they noticed that he was naked. He wore a torch light on his forehead.

Gratified and relieved to have found a saviour, Adendo and Serena followed the man closely, praying all the while.

The man led them through the thick foliage, slashing at trees that blocked their path. Finally, they reached a part of the jungle where the foliage was less dense and they could see their way through to a little stream. The man beckoned them to wade through it. They followed him shivering. As they walked away from the jungle, it seemed to have faded away into a large green mass fringed by red rocks. The rain began to lessen; drizzling in soft showers and light from the horizon shimmered on the stream.

Along the top of the long, wide bend in the river was a town. The river made a sweep here, and its main force struck the edge of the town, washing at some of the mud houses. It was particularly beautiful that evening, with the sun setting below the dark town. The clouds were golden-red, aflame with the brilliance of the sun that had travelled over the land and as the brilliance faded, a new moon appeared, tender and delicate.

"Follow this path to the Afiram plains' the man pointed to a pathway that lay beside the village. It is a long way but a straight route."

""We are very grateful." Adendo said enthusiastically. "Please accept this as a token of friendship." He removed his complimentary card and some money from his pocket and handed it to him.

The man smiled and waved at them. "Good luck."

They walked for many hours holding hands. The drizzle had ended and a lump appeared in Adendo['s throat as he saw the rainbow appear in the sky, filling it with many colours. Although, he was weary, the colours seemed to give him a new life, infusing him with hope and deep love – love for his creator, love for Serena and love for the world.

"Marry me, Serena." He couldn't help himself from saying the words.

Suddenly overcome by tenderness, Serena threw her arms around Adendo's neck. His nose was cold as it dug into her flesh and his breath was hot. Relaxing her embrace, she gazed at his masculine face - the thick eyebrows, nicely shaped nose, clean-shaven cheeks and shapely lips. She kissed each of these and replied.

"Yes, I will marry you Adendo."

Adendo felt his spirit expand. In spite of the circumstances that had led them here, he was very grateful for the fact that it had finally brought Serena to the point of agreeing to marry him. He had waited for this for twenty years!

"When can we get married?" Adendo asked impatiently.

"We would have to wait for at least two weeks. It would be exactly a year when I filed my divorce to Tenkora and it would be then be legally valid."

"I am sorry but we cannot wait till then, Serena" Adendo explained gently. "I know you may call this bigamy but I cannot take the chance the Tenkora might try again to separate us. We must get married by next week."

Serena looked up to Adendo's earnest face. "I have always tried to do what is right and I know it may be wrong not to wait but with you it feels so right – we have waited for so long!"

Adendo felt immensely happy with Serena's consent and run his hands all over her beautiful face as if he was playing with a flower. He fed her hunger for love with his touch then slowly kissed her on the mouth. Peace and light suddenly came over them and a sense of greater happiness they had never imagined before.

CHAPTER 12

Kofi Johnson catches the ball thrown at him by Haisu Chou and throws it effortlessly into the basketball net.

"You are good man, just like we were those days!"

"When we were in the board room trying to make impossibilities possible, there you were jumping around like a barbarous bulldog!"

Haisu Chou laughed out loud and patted Kofi on the back before continuing to bounce the ball:

"He is the man!" Haisu Chou chuckled as he ran off.

....

Kofi Johnson rubbed his chest gleefully, congratulating himself for the change of name to an Ashanti name. This was a name from one of the regions in a country in Africa. He had waited so long to confirm which country but he was now sure it was Ghana. This had happened during their year of return too. Now he had returned home and tagging along was his Chinese colleague. This man did not belong here the way he did. Or did he?

"All men come from Africa right? And they say hines and Africans are first cousins." Kofii puffed.

Ghana had the right kind of vision and energy he was looking for. As an Agibusiness professor who had completed his Ph.D. close to middle age, he was ready to implement his ideas in Africa, hopefully Ghana!

"What an opportunity!" He kept murmuring to himself as he boarded the plane and red Adendo's letter of invitation over again. He was being invited to start the AgriPower movement in Ghana to work side by side with Adendo. He was ready to start a logistics makeover! The African countries were young boys with many problems and a logistics makeover would turn the weaknesses into strengths and threats into opportunities. He was an African American entrepreneur born in America and he wanted to invest in Ghana. He was going back home to invest. His ancestors had come to America to struggle and now he and his children were freemen and he wanted his children to be a part of this energy whilst they were young. He had visited Ghana before as a student peace corp and had stayed there for five years. Now Love and nostalgia made him want to help Ghana in Agribusiness.

Kofi reminisced about how he established the Agribusiness club after he visited the Chief of the Sharma community.

"What can we do for you?" He had asked them.

"We want more technology to grow more food."

Kofi, who had just returned from an amazing smart manufacturing conference organized in Nigeria by his friend Haisu Chou had replied.

"I know the right man for you and there is a lot you can share."

Yes, they could offer Haisu Chou a lot of the plastics that was flying in the rubbish heap in the area because Haisu needed this for his recycling project. Haisu was also interested in Adendo's Agripower movement and it could all be pulled together.

"I can offer a lot in this our collaboration." Haisu Chou said out loudly and he turned to look at Adendo. Adendo walked to the chief and whispered something in his ear and then walked to stand beside Kofi and Haisu. It was as if something magical had taken place in the room.

After the meeting with the Sharma community, there was drumming and dancing and Haisu Chou joined Kofi and Adendo as they hit their chest triumphantly in dance.

"You are the man!" Kofi praised Haisu

"You bet! I gave my last few dollars to the farmer who helped me with my research at the botanical gardens"

"is that your only memory of Ghana? I am talking big dollars here! Do you remember the Ministerial conference at the luxurious hotel you are occupying now? That is now the real story of Ghana."

"no that is not the real story. The real story start with that poor farmer who has planted the new seeds that I gave to him from China and who would reap a whole plantation of the produce net year"

"What?"

Haisu Chou nodded at Adendo enthusiastically.

"Yes, that is my story – a cross-cultural collaboration between Ghana and China that is transformative."

Adendo suddenly seemed distracted:

"I have fought so hard for the voice of those fsrmers to be heard..."

"This is the man!" Kofi said emphatically looking Adendo straight in the eye. "It is smart manufacturing this time."

"I thought you said the same thing before he failed at the implementation of the IT technology in Liberia. " Adendo interjected jokingly.

"This time it is food" Kofi intervened.

"That is true, but we do not want any genetically modified food here oh so that even the chickens would be walking like this..." Adendo started to walk like a lame man in jest.

"No the lifestock in Ghana are vegetarians and after we feed them with what Haisu Chou is planning for the farms, they would walk like this.." Kofi began to mimick a lame man till they all broke out laughing and began to dance to the local drumming.

....

Serena quickly picked her call on the mobile phone when she recognized it was Adendo calling. She mad aa face at the deafening sound of drums and said to herself aloud:

"I really do not know who is worse – Adendo or Tenkora. They have both brought investors with such odd behaviors to Ghana. Well, let us give them a chance till we hear them at the Delico board room tomorrow."

....

Haisu Chou entered the board room in magnificent strides as is African boubou whirled around him in exaggerated style, made to look even more elegant by the ceiling fan that whirled it around. Haisu was pleased for the fan breeze as he had been sweating profusely for hours in the heat when he had stood outside. He pulled out his handkerchief to wipe his sweat as he walked awkwardly to stand in front of the audience.

He announced: "I have 3 plants for Agripower that can trasform Agriculture and Health in this African country."

The audience burst out laughing, much to the irritation of Haisu Chou. Kofi who previously had been walking sheepishly behind him was emboldened and walked to his side and tapped him gently on the shoulder:

"Africa is not a country but Ghana is – you are in Ghana." He corrected with a smile.

"And Ghana is ready for my investment, No?" Haisu Chou asked in a puzzled manner.

"Ghana is the gateway to Africa" Kofi declared.

The audience clapped heartily.

"Agripower!" Haisu Chou cheered Adendo on with a fist in the air,,

"Agripower" Adendo smiled enthusiastically, giving Haisu Chou a warm embrace.

"I love this man!"

CHAPTER 13

The little path by the lake, which extended for miles was a beautiful spot, secluded and far away. The wedding took place at this Palm grove resort on a sunny Saturday afternoon. Only immediate members of the family and a few close friends witnessed the exchange of vows.

Her cascading wedding gown of sparkling white silk was symbolic of their love –unrestrained and flowing. Her eyes reflected the diamonds that glittered around her neck – embers glow with a deep fire of love. The marigold flowers she held in her hands glowed with a lustrous richness, mirroring the sweet blossoming of inner joy.

Soon, it was done. Serena Tiko, who had become Serena Babanda, was now Serena Bilay. Adendo and his wife stared at each other in amazement and joy.

It seemed to Adendo that Serena looked more beautiful than ever - not because of her gown or jewellery or the flowers, but because of the beauty that shone from her eyes. Her whole face was lit up with the love and goodness that was representative of her life.

There was a blessing in the air, a love that covered everything.

They spent their honeymoon at a secluded hotel with beautiful scenery near the Afiram plains. On the first morning, they went to the top of a romantic hillside called Lover's place. Here, they wandered through the Lover's park and they took a ferryboat ride to the romantic poolside, where they sat to have their lunch. They spent magical hours making wonderful plans for their love.

It was a magnificent moment when looking with immense love into her eyes, Adendo took out a velvet red case and handed it to Serena.

"For the woman who will share my bed, my life and my dreams." He pronounced. He watched as Serena opened the case with delight and appreciation. It was a set of dazzling sapphire earrings and necklace filled with rainbows.

"Oh thank you so much. They are so beautiful!" She said with a breathless rush of joy and tears. She smiled – that soft, lovely smile, which he loved so much and threw her arms around his neck to kiss him deeply.

"This is a symbol of the new memories we are going to create – the rainbow after the storm." Adendo promised.

....

Chief Inspector Kat looked appreciatingly at the bank statement he had received with the cooperation of Chief Accountant of the Trade Centre. He had been chosen as the head of the Board of enquiry into the case accusing the Trade Centre of corrupt dealings because he was a wizard with figures and could read a lot of meaning into them. However, he didn't have to be an expert to tell from the bank statement he was now holding, he could tell that people's money had been misappropriated. The several debits on the account could not be substantiated.

Some men would do anything to be rich – to have wealth, luxurious cars and women. But that had never been his way. He just worked hard and tried to get along. It had been his duty for the past few years to put assist in putting offenders behind bars. Someone was going to hang!

Tenkora greeted the commissioner of police with gracious apology.

"Please forgive me for the delay in honouring your request for this meeting. I have been so busy over the past week trying to catch up with some business in the Afiram plains."

"Ah Afiram plains. Is that where you plan to set up the cocoa processing factory?"

"Yes. Yes, and plans are far advanced. We just had a slight setback but things would soon be on track."

"Hmm. Honourable Babanda, is it true that as a result of this and other projects, you have received substantial payments – bribes?"

"That is ridiculous. This is libelous accusations."

"Perhaps you do not know that we have been investigating some shady deals you have been involved in with some foreign investors and that the facts are being revealed."

"What facts? This is sensational journalism. Leave me alone."

"I will for now but remember the state will not leave you alone, when we have completed oru investigations."

"Show me the proof."

"See you in court, Honourable Babanda." The commissioner of police stated flatly and made his exit.

Tenkora's forehead broke out in cold sweat. How on earth had anybody got to know about the details of his dealings with Tortison, he wondered. He suddenly felt lost and confused. Tortison had been bitten by a snake and was in hospital and Adendo was in hiding with Serena. His plans had gone haywire. But he needed to find Serena – to convince her to come back to him – to give the documents on the Afiram plains. Tomorrow, it would be a year exactly since she had filed the divorce papers and though he had not signed the papers it would be legally valid.

He could not wait for tomorrow to come – he had to find Serena when she was still legally married to him!

Tenkora's intention of finding Serena was stalled by an angry crowd of indignant investors who had invested their money in the 'CP fund'. He did not have the opportunity to leave the gates of the Trade Centre in his jeep. The mob surrounded his car, singing excitedly. It was an angry song, curiously harmonized, with no resolving cadences to set the hearers at rest. The angry voices rang: *"You can fool some of the people some of the time, but you can not make fools of all the people all the time. We no go sit down make you cheat us everyday!"*

Tenkora hated and feared the truth of the rioters words. He got down bravely from his jeep and cut into their song with a loud voice: "Please have patience with us. We are honest people and we live by our word."

The indignant rioters who immediately began to throw the stones, which they held in their fists and charged at him. Tenkora began to run, fearing they were going to trample him. The sound of pounding footsteps behind him roared in his ears. The anger of the crowd seemed fiercer as they ran. Their reeling strength snatched at Tenkora's energy and before long he was pulled into their mist and he was forced to face them all at once. His heart laboured painfully. Fear made him stumble, lose his balance and fall to his knees. He raised his arms to shield his head as stones and jeers were hurled at him.

He felt a sharp pain shoot through his skull. He had been hit by one of the stones! It had been aimed straight at his head, and it had hit him!

Nightmare. None of this is happening, is happening.....

Through the wild whirl of his pain, another stone hit his back. Darkness swarmed at him and he reeled to the ground, falling facedown in the sand. Everything around him suddenly became too much for him. They overwhelmed his perceptions, passed beyond his senses into stark darkness.

He was waking up, though he felt more as if he was dropping into grogginess. Gradually, he became able to identify where he was. He lay in bed with white sheets covering him up to the chin. He could hardly move. All his joints seemed numb. Somehow the fact that he couldn't move his hands did not seem significant. His heart was too hot with other emotions. Suddenly, he made out two figures standing at the foot of the bed. One of them was a woman in white - a nurse. As he tried to focus on her, she said, "Doctor - he's regaining consciousness."

The doctor was a middle-aged man. His eyes were sharp and his moustache shielded his heavy lips, which broke into a smile as Tenkora opened his eyes. The doctor approached along the side of the bed, pulled up Tenkora's eyelids and shone a small light at his pupils. With an effort, Tenkora focused on the light. The doctor nodded and put his flashlight away.

Tenkora swallowed at the dryness of his throat. "Where am I?" He asked.

"You're in hospital." The doctor held his face close to that of Tenkora, speaking quietly and calmly. "You were brought here after you were attacked during the riot. You've been unconscious for over six hours."

Tenkora lifted his head and nodded to show that he understood.

"Good," said the doctor. "I suppose I should keep you under observation for a day or two. Then I'll let you go home if you want to."

Tenkora gave no answer. He lay still, only wishing to nestle in his pillow for as long as he could. As he remembered the humiliating scene of the mob attack over again, his shoulders

shook and tears trickled down his face. His dreams and hopes collapsed with an explosion that made the blood roar in his ears.
My reputation has gone down the drain!

....

As always on weekends, Adendo awakened long before Serena. After he had showered and dressed, he stood over the bed and as she moved slightly, like a kitten stretching and then curling back into a cozy sleep, he bent down to kiss her lovely lips. It wasn't 7 a.m. yet but the sun was already warm.

Serena tasted Adendo's sweet kiss on her lips and stretched pleasurably. All her senses were

suddenly heightened as she woke up. The world seemed brighter, more vivid, and music rang in her heart with such purity. The morning sun caressed her skin with tingling delicacy and her sleep felt luxurious.

Serena flung the bed covers off her and sprung out of bed to hug Adendo. But quite suddenly, she felt sick in the stomach and needed to throw up. She rushed off to the bathroom. She returned to the bedroom, hardly able to walk. Realising she looked rather pale, Adendo put her back in bed and propped her up with pillows.

"I have a terrible migraine and I feel cold." She announced. Adendo rushed to the telephone to call the family doctor, who arrived promptly.

"My dear, you are pregnant." The doctor declared when he came in to see Serena.

Serena was suddenly filled with a newly gained energy, her heart full of excitement.

"Pregnant!" Adendo exclaimed, "pregnant! How wonderful!" His hands reached for Serena's waist, encircling her, then tightened with crushing force and hauled her against his full length. "Oh I'm so happy!"

In the next few moments of joyful silence, they gazed at each other, both realizing the wonderful gift of love they were soon to receive.

Very soon, the news of Serena's pregnancy spread among the extended family. It became the consensus of opinion that her former husband, Tenkora, was truly sterile. They began to speak of Serena's marriage in the most admiring of terms. "He is such a strong man." They would say of Adendo. "The epitome of virility combined with amiability."

To Adendo, the joy of once again becoming a father overwhelmed him. For the weeks ensuing, he withheld nothing from Serena and gave her everything – his love, his attention and many gifts to delight her.

Adendo appeared in the bedroom just as the conversation was ending. The soft uncertainty in Serena's voice, and the telephone cord, tangled and twisted by her anxioufs fingers, told him that she had been speaking to Auntie Tami.

"How is Auntie Tami?" He asked when she replaced the receiver and looked up at him.

"She is fine."

"And what is the latest new?"

"Tenkora is in trouble. The news of the failure of the Cocoa processing factory is all over town and he is to be taken to court. But what is worse, Alima has just had a baby…."

"That is very good news for Tenkora." Adendo exclaimed.

No, not good news... The baby is a white baby! It is not Tenkora's baby and he is yet to find out."

"Oh my God!" Adendo exclaimed. "What punishment for the way he treated you, just because he wanted children. Tenkora should have faced the fact that he was the sterile party." Adendo pondered gravely. The ancient feelings of rejection triggered as Serena remembered the uneasiness of the past but she quickly brushed it aside to look forward to the hopefulness of the future. Now she was pregnant and with Adendo's baby!

"Let's go and sit in the garden." She held Adendo's hand and tugged it gently.

The Serena gardens welcomed them with its sweet fragrance from the flowers, which glowed with hues of gold and red. Climbers stretched their tendrils, embracing the trees and spilling their blossoms in gigantic loops around the garden.

Bathed in the light of the sun, Adendo sprawled in the garden chair with a smile on his face as he stretched his hands to touch the trees. He looked towards the sun with his eyes closed, feeling its rays against his face. In that moment another familiar sensation swept across his body - a particular warmth and feeling of well-being. He reached out for Serena who was sitting by his side.

"I love you." He whispered to her, his head on her stomach, as if to listen to the heartbeat of their baby. "Oh God, I love you so!".

Serena smiled. She could feel the baby inside her growing, changing and developing so fast. Her life was elevated with this new relation to another life inside her, so close and sharing her body. She felt a certain gentleness and from this tenderness, she felt as if she was moving on through a deeper life of her own. Serena relished in Adendo's pleasure. Lines of character was growing on his face and becoming more dominant. There was however a developing air of simplicity around him with this new knowledge of love. It was as if they were both just beginning to fall in love with life.

....

There were many people in the courtroom early on the sunny Tuesday morning, eager to hear the verdict of the case, Babanda versus the state. The courtroom was a modern one, fully carpeted with new furnishings made of cold dark wood. It was referred to as the 'modern fast-track court'. The group of people sitting in the first row to the right were reporters and Tenkora watched them cynically as they looked eagerly on his case. Tenkora was replete in his one hundred dollars custom-made suit, light blue lace shirt and gold tie. He looked terrific and felt convinced that he was in good hands.

Lawyer Tega had assure him that they were going to win the case. He was good and had been well paid. He would damage Chief Inspector Kat's efforts and inject a large dose of uncertainty into the legal mechanism. Should the case begin to go against him, Lawyer Tega would establish a case for a possible reversal in a higher court.

Lawyer Tega had the gait of a boxer - thickening around the middle and light on his feet. Even sitting, he appeared as if he was ready to spring. Lawyer Tega went on for five minutes with no loss of wind. Sleek in wording and in tone, he invoked the constitution to prove that what Tenkora had done was not against the law but carefully considered and done for a purpose. He raked the opposing lawyer with a fiery warning glance that told them he was only getting warmed up.

The opposition lawyer, Lawyer Timi, was also an extremely eloquent lawyer, well known for his glibness. His speech silenced the court to pensive thought:

"What is the use of a Minister of State's brilliant academic record and vast experience if he certifies that a defective contract is OK, because he is offered a fat bribe? The contract's defect may come to light after some years; Great harm has been done to the community. With all his abilities, knowledge and experience,

Honourable Babanda lacked something vital - correct qualities and attitudes, in particular integrity and courage."

With his confidence a bit shaken by Laywer Timi's powerful speech, Tenkora felt suddenly frightened when called to the witness stand. He lowered his eyes as he took his oath. Then he turned to face Lawyer Timi who looked extremely indifferent to his agony, his pose aggressive and his gestures hostile.

"Tenkora Babanda, what exactly is your association with the two investors, Mr. Tortison and Mr. Rizo?"

"We were parties to the signing of a contract for the importation of farming machinery into Ghana."

"Mr. Babanda, when you were signing the contract, did you by chance notice that there had been a clause 27 inserted into the contract, which had not originally been part of the initial contract?"

"I did but ….but I was blackmailed into signing it." Tenkora said lowering his head.

"Well, after this blackmail, why did you then again associate yourself with the same rogues to dupe innocent citizens in you country by setting up a fake Cocoa Processing fund that had no intention of paying investors back their money."

Tenkora felt the rapid beating of his heart. Surely, it was beating too fast?

"I honestly thought that the fund will yield enough profit to set up a Cocoa Processing factory and repay investments. We were just unlucky."

"Mr. Babanda," Lawyer Timi continued in a condemning voice. "Are you denying that you connived with Mr. Tortison and Mr. Rizo to set up the fund to enrich yourself under the guise of making money for the people and setting up the cocoa-processing factory?"

Tenkora's lawyer was on his feet. "Objection your honour. There is no reason why Mr. Babanda should be asked to incriminate himself."

"Overruled." The judge answered immediately "The question is in place."

"I was genuinely seeking to help my country ……."

"And yourself?"

"Well…"

"Let me repeat to you Mr. Babanda and to the court an excerpt from the opinion of the first President of this country." He paused and looked around. "Think not what your country can do for you but what you can do for your country." He turned abruptly to Tenkora. "Would you agree with the First President's point of view, Mr. Babanda?"

His lawyer was on his feet again. "I object your honour. The question calls for my client's opinion on matters that are irrelevant and vague."

"Your honour!" The lawyer Tega protested in a now thundering tone. "It is essential that the court knows the once trusted Minister of State's point of view on moral issues."

"Objection overruled."

"Do you agree with the First President Mr. Babanda?" The lawyer repeated.

"It is a very general statement but I would say that I agree with him."

"Why did you decide to rob your country of its meagre resources in order to enrich yourself?"

Lawyer Tega came to Tenkora's rescue, deciding to use his last triumph card – that of soliciting sympathy from the public. He narrated how Tenkora had been blackmailed by Tortison and Rizo and had been forced into entering illicit dealings, which he had tried hard to overturn in the favour of his nation. It was as though the lawyer was on stage and those around him were his audience. Knowing that his client's life depended on it, he put up an excellent act.

Lawyer Timi's next question however threw him off.

Why was this information kept secret until now?

As the case of Babanda versus the State progressed, the publicity in the newspapers exceeded Tenkora's worst fears. There were pictures of him and the headlines ran: "Corrupt Minister of Trade and Industry soon to be jailed."

There seemed no one around to comfort him. Alima was now in the hospital after a prolonged labour. That was his only source of hope at the moment. That he would soon have a baby boy who would look up to him as father, who would give back to him that self-esteem the masses wanted to rob him of.

Feelings of regret swarmed over him. Why had he allowed Tortison and Rizo to manipulate him? Maybe he should have informed the President about the blackmail situation and asked for his help instead of going along with Tortison and Rizo's plans. After all, they couldn't have forced him to set up the CP fund. That was not part of the contract.

As the court resumed for the verdict to be read, Tenkora stood on his feet to listen to the verdict, his mind ablaze. In all of his inner turmoil, he created a little space of hope in his heart for his baby boy.

"....We declare Tenkora Babanda guilty! He is to be sentenced to fifteen years imprisonment and to pay back an amount of one million five hundred dollars he has confiscated from the state."

There was a roar in the courtroom, then wild applause and loud booing. Tenkora slumped back, eyes shut. One arm rolled limply over the arm of his chair. Lawyer Goho oozed sympathy.

Tenkora almost sank to his feet but he remained standing straight for his son. Suddenly, his mind went into oblivion.

CHAPTER 14

Alima sat up in the hospital bed and stared at her baby. It was almost completely white part from the slightly kinky hair. Tortison had rejected this baby and so probably would Tenkora. Her poor baby would be fatherless. Maybe Tenkora would adopt him when he came to the realisation that he could not produce children. But did she really want her baby to have a convict for a father?

What would Tenkora do when he found out? She wondered. Would he beat her and take from her all the gifts he had bought her? Well, maybe it was a good thing that he is soon to be put behind bars.

She was surprised at her own composure.

She started as she looked up to see Tenkora escorted by two policemen, walking towards the hospital bed. The expectant look on his face made her want to disappear. He walked as if in slow motion. His eyes were fixed on the baby on her lap and he reached out for it as if he was reaching out to hold the one thread of hope in his life.

"A w-white baby?" He stammered confused as he held the baby in his hands.

"Didn't it ever occur to you that Tortison may be making love to your wife, while you were busy seeking public favour?" She asked in a gloating voice, happy to destroy his illusions about a man in whom he had placed so much trust. "I needed to have a child and you could never give me one. The sad thing about you Tenkora was that you would never admit you were infertile. You wouldn't even make the effort to see the doctor. They could have salvaged you." Her voice cracked.

The strange voice that emitted from his lips was far-off and confined. None of his escorts recognised the shriek to come from him until it grew louder and he yelled as if in deep pain, throwing his wrists in the air. His face was that of gnashing despair with swollen veins and a frenzied look in his eyes. He uttered a long guttural sigh and fell on the floor writhing.

The policemen were bewildered as they tried to get him off the floor. He seemed to have more strength than the two of them together as he wrestled with them violently.

"He is going insane." They announced. The once derisive look on their faces had now changed to that of deep sympathy.

Adendo stood in front of the High court judge trying to make him understand his case.

"Justice Archi, we have received news that Tenkora is in mental trauma. I would appeal that his sentence be suspended till his condition improves."

"I am sorry, I think I have made myself clear in this matter. We are not going to drop charges against Tenkora Babanda."

"I am not suggesting that you drop the charges, merely to suspend his sentence till he gets better. This is not the time to send him to prison."

"He has wronged the state and the jury has pronounced him guilty. There is nothing I can do. The case is over."

"The man is in hospital on the brink of insanity, for God's sake!"

"We have no choice Mr. Bilay. Tenkora Babanda has stepped out of line too often. And why are you trying to defend him? He tried to destroy you, remember?"

"Try to understand, the man is suffering already."

"Tenkora Babanda has gone mad." A voice interrupted their conversation. Adendo turned to see a policeman followed by a nursing sister. Adendo sank on the bench, a sharp pang of empathy running through his heart at this announcement. Despite all he had done to him, Tenkora had once been his mentor and friend. Now Tenkora was mad.

Justice Archi dropped his pen. "So, he has chosen the lesser indictment – madness over years of suffering in prison."

"Nature had judged and sentenced him. There was no need for a second one." Adendo pleaded.

Justice Archi looked thoughtfully at Adendo, digesting the gravity of his words.

....

At the one-year anniversary celebration of the 'Agripower' co-operative, which coincided with the yam festival at the Afiram plains, Adendo was impressed as he assessed the results of all the hard work in the Antelope plains. It was amazing. The town had transformed into a very different town Centre with modern community houses, delineated by well-mapped out streets leading to the large farms. There was a large school by the roadside where the youth had access to evening tuition in various subjects. The youth had flooding the town in drones, taking their place on the farms. The success of this initiative was being recognised, referred to and learnt from by many towns in Ghana.

Boisterous laughter rang from the villagers assembled at the park where the festive occasion was taking place. The excitement that rang in their voices was something else. Adendo called it land fever. It was definitely contagious and made him feel the same restlessness of spirit as he hastened to join them for the yam festival.

The yam festival was a festival held in honour of the mother earth after the harvest season between August and September. It was a festival that emphasized good fortune, good health, posterity and prosperity. On display was every kind of produce that the land had yielded – green plantains and yellow bananas, garden eggs, tomatoes, palm-nuts, oranges, pineapples, pawpaw, yams, maize – all filled shining brass trays and golden calabashes.

A pleasing arrangement of indigenous craft such as traditional baskets, pots and bamboo products also adorned the park. Acrobats, colourfully dressed walked around on long stilts, showing off their skill. Young girls dressed in elaborate traditional costumes made of colourful, richly textured cloth, carried baskets of lush tropical fruits onto the grounds.

A row of Ghanaian flags surrounding the park caught the breeze and swayed in rhythm to the festive music. Colourful ethnic dances performed to the accompaniment of deafening drums welcomed the guests - dignitaries, industrialists, academics and other invitees.

The miscellaneous crowd, all dressed in colourful traditional costume looked a singular festivity. The men were dressed in long smocks and hats with intricately woven patterns and the women wore flowing long skirts with blouses, complete with headgear. The chiefs in their colourful palanquins, followed by their pageantry were dressed in heavy gold-plait necklaces and rings of the most intricate artistry.

The earth vibrated with deep resounding sounds from drums from which stirred deep choruses in the Ghanaian soul. Called to life, seven vibrant figures became alive with the sound of the drums. They met with bursting energy and wove and interwove in a vibrant dance. Full-throated voices backed the drums with their sweet melody.

Serena watched with pride as Adendo climbed the podium to address the farmers.

Adendo bowed his head to the gathering and the people responded with loud cheers and vigorous clapping. As Adendo stood facing the crowd, the place suddenly became quiet, the air electric. The crowd strained forward to hear Adendo's speech.

When the last bit of clapping had rippled through the enthusiastic hands of the audience, Adendo began: "I feel like the oldest man in this room because I have lived to see my vision come true."

The applause and cheers started to build up again.

"I will like to express my feelings at this moment in the words written by our great ancestor, the first President of Ghana." After a momentary pause, he placed his words into the welcoming silence like a rough and rare jewel:

This is our precious land
God's great gift to us
Legacy obtained through the blood of our forefathers,
It is now our turn
We must continue to redeem our great land
Arise patriot! Arise to achieve wealth and prosperity
for your land!

The words made Adendo quiver and his heart wept with unreserved joy.

....

The corridor in the psychiatric wing of the hospital was painted bright, sickly yellow and there was a strong scent of disinfectant that wafted through the air. Tenkora sat on the

149

bed at the furthermost corner, his eyes wandering anxiously around the room. He wished for privacy, away from the nurses who watched his every move, listening to the words that spewed from his mouth when he broke his silence so they could report to the doctor the progress of his insanity. They would occasionally allowed him to pace along the corridor and he cherished those moments because they were his private moments when he could think about Serena.

Serena! Her name flowed and floated in his mind as he recalled wondrous memories of her love. The sun was falling on him through the window, like his own golden dream. Then the memory eluded him, dancing away, out of reach of his floating mind. Then a new image of Serena began to materialize, close enough to touch, to hear, to see!

She looked so beautiful in a long, silk blue dress, with her hair falling around her face in rich curls. She wore glittering jewellery around her neck and she looked happy! It dawned on Tenkora that he, who was once her husband, had never seen her look so happy. This was the image he wanted to hold, to love, to cherish, not to cast away as he had done. He reached out his arms, imploring her to enter them, to entwine her arms around his neck – become his once again. His arms froze in mid air, falling disappointedly and then curling into a hard fist as she stood indifferent to his need. Was it too late? Had Adendo taken her completely away from him?

"Serena!" He whispered, yearning to say soft, gentle words to her – words that would woo her once again. Serena looked up at him, her eyes filled with compassion as she followed his gaze to her hands that was adorned with Adendo's ring. She waited, expectant, as he made the discovery. Tears threatened to flood her eyes. Tenkora had grown lean and looked like a lost schoolboy in plain, drub clothes and overgrown hair. She swayed to the side, suddenly dizzy with heartfelt sympathy. She turned to Adendo, who was holding her hand.

"Sit down, Serena." Adendo guided her to sit on the chair facing Tenkora's bed.

"How are you, Tenkora?" Serena asked in a low, consoling voice.

"Serena .... I am well." He replied after a long pause.

Listening to his unsteady voice, watching him, Serena saw a Tenkora she had never known before. There was no dominance, no arrogance, and no words of reproach and blame. - only a stoic acceptance of a miserable situation. She turned aside, her eyes full of tears that rolled down and she did not attempt to hide it. Adendo felt a rush of emotion as he saw Serena cry and he reached out his hands to grasp hers. The pained look in Tenkora's eyes as he beheld their closeness made Adendo recoil. Adendo turned to face the man who was once his mentor, protégé and friend. Tenkora's eyes mirroring a torrent of recriminations, and he stood as if being sentenced a second time, facing a firing squad and steeled for the bullets that would shatter his heart.

"Serena and I are married." He stated flatly. "But I did not take Serena away from you. I only took what you discarded, which was what I so much longed for."

"What did you gain by taking her away from me?" Tenkora asked Adendo bitterly.

"I love Serena and I guess I have learnt lessons, which if you had learnt earlier would have sent you to great heights."

Tenkora's heart churned with angry energy. "No, it was I who sent you to great heights! I am responsible for your bank account, your social status, your name!" He shouted at Adendo.

"You took all that away, remember?" Adendo shouted back as painful memories flooded in.

"And you took my wife! What has she taught you – all that she learnt from me?" Tenkora's nostrils flared and his chest heaved faster.

"You abandoned Serena when you felt she was not meeting your expectations. But I learnt through all that that a man who respects his wife will conduct his life properly so as to please her and by conducting his life properly, he would rise in the world with his wife as a source of strength and refuge."

Tenkora's eyes flashed at Adendo indignantly as emotions of recrimination tore at him.

"Did I not set you on the path to rid our people of their poverty and desperation, prevent the youth from flooding out of the country in drones to find their fortune abroad? Did I not give you the vision for economic prosperity through an agricultural transformation?"

"And yet when you found the opportunity, you decided to take advantage of these very same people. Economic growth the way we once talked about it was not growth in our own pockets. It represented much more than that."

Adendo paused for a while but could not withhold thoughts that were gnawing at him. "Where were the moral overtones you once upheld, Tenkora? You threw them all away and sided with cheap hustlers and con men."

"No! No! I fought with determination and against great odds to turn Ghana into a great nation." Tenkora protested vehemently as he recalled his thwarted dreams.

Adendo reached out to grasp his shaking hands. "Yes, I longed for the day when together we would behold the great goal. It was a vast, shark-infested ocean yet we survived because of principle. What went wrong Tenkora?"

Powerful emotions, dangerous and damaging, tore at Tenkora. His eyes flashed with helpless resentment and hot tears filled his eyes at this condemnation from Adendo. Then suddenly, the thundering emotions subsided and he felt emptiness. The tears poured out of his eyes in wrenching sobs that shook his body and tore themselves from him in painful torrents. Serena threw her hands on Adendo's shoulder and squeezed it tight to indicate that he had said enough.

"Let's leave now." She said. "Tenkora needs some rest."

The nurse seemed to be of the same opinion as she came closer to put Tenkora to bed, covering him with blankets as he shivered.

"We will be back. You will be in our prayers." Adendo said gravely to Tenkora as they turned to leave.

Tenkora watched on helplessly as Adendo and Serena quietly exited the ward. He shivered even more violently as feelings of remorse washed over him and bitter thoughts hammered at his heart like hard, ugly nails:

Oh how could I have failed so badly? I was so fascinated by money and power. Now my frustration has become a curse. I have become a bitter and cynical man, made bankrupt by a political purge and betrayed by my wife. I have played with politics and found nothing. People's words and gestures have degraded me. They have forgotten that I devoted a great part of my career to the improvement of agriculture in Ghana. I am now at war with myself. My mind says one thing and my heart says another. My life is now empty, dull and without much significance. My sorrow is not only remorse, but also the feeling of suddenly being left alone. I have never had this kind of sorrow before. What am I to do? How am I to get over it? Adendo, you were once a friend, I'll admit, almost my brother but for your competition with everything that lay dear to my heart. I did you great wrong and I hope to God that you will forgive me. Don't we forgive everything of a friend? Yes, forgive selfishness and guile?

Serena, you were once my woman - a woman in every sense of the word. I wished I had understood you then, when you were once mine. I had so many arguments against you, aggravated by the fact that I thought you could give me no children. Now you are lingering in the arms of another man. You have given him what I could not get from you...... Does he kiss you better than I did? Do your bodies meet in perfume, in sweat and lingering passion?.... Kiss me Serena, kiss me and call me by my name.

At the maternity block at the Ridge Clinic, Adendo heard Serena shrieking and moaning and he prayed for her life with no concern for that of the baby. All he longed for was an end to her suffering. The screams followed each other quickly and reached a crescendo. Adendo could take no more and rushed into the maternity room. He saw Serena's burning face, full of pain, biting her lips to keep back the tears. The doctor frowned at him, looking sterner than ever. He saw it as his cue to leave the room.

Adendo paced along the corridor as the minutes went by, then the hours till he lost all sense of time, growing extremely tense with apprehension. "Lord save Serena and the baby." he prayed. He finally gathered enough courage to peep once again into the delivery room. The doctor beckoned him to enter. Serena was making muffled sounds as she strained to push out the baby. The doctor further beckoned him to assist in the delivery process. With nervous hands, Adendo joined the doctor to hold the baby as Serena gave her final push. His heart contracted with happiness and melted within him.

Adendo could not believe his eyes as he held two sticky babies in his arms – a boy and a girl! Serena felt herself transported into a world of such luminous happiness as she held the babies. Tears of joy dropped from her eyes. Falling on his knees, Adendo dropped to the side of Serena and held her hands tightly, raining it with kisses.

"I love you Serena." he whispered and his voice, mingled with the persistent cry of the baby rang like golden chords in her ears.

Serena looked down at the babies and laughed through her tears. Holding their babies was now giving her life a meaning it had lacked for so long. She would give them all the love that had been locked in her heart for so many years!

....

Aunt Tami slid subdued through the narrow rows of chairs arranged for the naming ceremony of Serena's twins. For a fat woman with a huge butt, she was unusually silent in movement. The surprising turn of events had tamed her. Imagine Serena and Adendo getting married, and having twins! Wonders would never end! She rolled her eyes to heaven and stopped short when she saw an even more surprising scene. He poverty-stricken farmers she had seen at the Ghana Independence day's celebration stood at the side of the room dressed in splendid attire, the colors of the flag. Each one of the twenty or so farmers had a smile on their face. The couple must have come into some money she concluded until the next turn of events answered her questions with revelations about this happy ending.

As the naming ceremony proceeded, the baby girl was named 'Adin' after Serena's mother, meaning 'harmony' and the baby boy was named 'Mdou' after Adendo's great-grandfather, who was a great warrior, meaning 'prosperity'. Adendo stood proudly in the center of the living room and proclaimed:

"I would like to inform all of you that the names of our children tie in with the values of our Industrial Park, which we have built together – harmony and prosperity. So you all have a stake in the lives of these young ones." Adendo raised his hands in the air dramatically.

"Agripower!" one farmer shouted out.

Mrs Azuri and Dr. Egare held hands and closed their eyes as if in prayer. Other members of the Agricultural Marketing board exchanged glances as they beheld this pose. There was a fever going round and every one in the room seemed to be catching it – even the babies as they cried excitedly.

"Agripower!" everyone in the room shouted out, "Agripower".

Serena smiled back at Mrs Zuzu who was making ogling faces at her, overcome with joy.